Wrong Bias

Wrong Bias

CP Wolf

Chapter 1

Cliff Doyle frowned and glanced, yet again, at the large digital clock located at the top right-hand corner of the imposing and impressive new scoreboard. He inaudibly mouthed the time it displayed, '9.20'. He shouldn't have been surprised as only moments before it had displayed 9.19. His eyes turned back to scan the scene before him. More than thirty people, all over 55 years of age with many nearer to a hundred than 55, were either wandering around or seated at tables in small groups. The joy and pure relief to be out and about after a long weekend, either spent in virtual solitude or having to put up with the noise of visiting rowdy grandchildren, were clearly visible on their animated faces. They were now wrapped up in their comfort blanket of the Monday morning winter open triples bowls league. Surprisingly, or maybe not, the winter league there was even more popular than its summer counterpart. Maybe that was because many bowled outdoors on a lawn green in one of the numerous local villages, or perhaps the lure of spending as much time as possible in a sun-drenched garden attracted the more green-fingered amongst them. Whatever the reason for its winter popularity, these people were always determined to defy any adverse weather conditions, even on a murky and rainy day such as that Monday in November.

Soon, the friendly rivalry, at least at the beginning of each match, would start, but for now they were basking in the security that this regular event afforded, giving them a much-needed social start to every week. At 9.30 the battles would commence, with 24 of them representing their various teams, such as 'The Dregs', 'The Wickies' or 'The Supremes', with both pride and sportsmanship. These matches would be played on the middle four rinks of the well-appointed facility. Those not picked for that week would 'roll up' and play fun games on the two outside rinks. They did not want to stay at home and miss the ritual that was Monday morning.

Even though he knew who, and what, he was looking for Cliff couldn't help but be confused by the commonality of those around him. Virtually everyone, save the balding, had hair in one shade of grey or pure white, and they were all wearing predominantly white shirts, as required by the club for their league matches, or the new Daventry Eagles club shirt itself – white with natty asymmetrical red and black flashes on one shoulder. Amongst this sea of white, Cliff could not locate the green epaulets nor the striking Fedora hat, favoured by his teammate Paddy Cullen.

'He's still not here,' he said, without looking at the person sitting next to him. 'He is never this late. You know how much he hates queuing for that bloody card machine.'

Charlie 'Chas' Findus stared at the line of six people standing in front of the office window. Each of them clinging onto their credit or debit card, desperately hoping that the 'tap' facility would work. He knew that at least fifty percent of them would need to refer to the bit of paper they had secreted on their person, should they be asked to enter the dreaded PIN number. 'Yes, it's not like him at all,' replied Chas, checking his neatly coiffured hair again. 'It is his turn to buy the coffees afterwards, and he'd be mortified to leave us in the lurch.'

Cliff checked his phone knowing that the signal strength was almost non-existent in the buildings. It's so frigging annoying,' he commented. 'We shouldn't have to sign on to the bloody guest wi-fi every time. What's the password again?' He was tapping on his mobile's screen, clearly trying to open "settings".

'Calm down, Cliff,' smiled Chas, knowing how easily wound-up Cliff could get. 'He knows the signal is crap here and would have rung the landline.'

'That's true,' said Cliff, putting his phone back down, 'and I've not heard it ring since we've been here. Anyway, Dave would have let us know, had he called.' With that he looked at the diminutive form of Dave Hedge, the steward for the morning, who was trying to remain calm as old Lenny Batts was repeatedly trying to present his card to the wrong end of the card reader. In the end, Dave's patience gave up and he snatched the card and did it himself. Lenny took the card back, not knowing whether to be thankful or annoyed. In the end he sheepishly put his wallet into his trouser pocket and turned to go towards the Gentlemen's toilets. 'Prostrate trouble or blood pressure tablets,' mused Cliff. 'If only urine were a valuable commodity. It would make getting old worth while.' Being an ex-foreign languages teacher, Cliff prided himself on his use of the subjunctive.

'The way I see it we have two options,' Chas was now in full problem-solving mode. 'Either we get Murray to play,' Chas pointed at Murray, their team captain who was going through a bowling crisis and preferred not to play competitively at the moment, 'or …..'. Without having to finish his alternative scenario, Cliff fully understood and followed Chas' redirected gaze towards another man who was sitting on his own near the café counter.

'But I don't want to play,' the man whined, like a four-year-old being told he had to go to bed. 'And it's not my turn anyway. I'm only here to watch and support,' he continued, pulling at his white goatee beard.

'Bollocks!' Cliff countered. 'We all know you're here to see Judith. And you can support us by playing, you old lech! Murray isn't up for playing today, and Judith will still be here when we've finished. I'll even buy you a coffee.'

Judith Fletcher was the very amiable and slightly flirtatious café manager, and Roy Grimble, who was in the process of going through his fourth divorce, had clearly marked this younger woman down as a potential candidate for Mrs Grimble number five.

'And a slice of lemon drizzle cake,' said Roy, playing the childish role for all it was worth.

'Only if you bowl well and we win,' replied Cliff.

'Well, that ain't going to happen,' laughed Chas, clapping Roy on the shoulder.

…………….

'What took you so long?' Roy demanded, as Cliff carefully placed a mug of tea on the John Smith's beer mat in front of him. This always seemed ironic as they had changed over to Timothy Taylor bitter well before the pandemic. Yet, there still seemed to be a never-ending supply of these mats from their previous bitter supplier. 'If I didn't know you better I'd think you were trying to muscle in on my territory,' he continued.

'Oh, do shut up,' responded Cliff. 'In fact, stuff your cake hole with this. I've just heard something quite worrying from Judith.' And with that he plopped a paper plate with a slice of lemon drizzle cake on it in front of his rather annoying friend.

'Oi!' Chas chimed in. How does he get cake? We just got hammered by 'The Gerry Hattricks' over there. And Roy was as useful as a chocolate teapot.' As if on cue, the aforementioned trio, Gerry Taylor, Jerry Naismith and Geraldine Peacock all approaching their tenth decade, and with Jerry requiring a bowling aid due to his Parkinson's, walked by at the same glacial pace at which they played bowls.

Cliff silently counted to ten, trying to temper the barbed reply which wanted to leap from his tongue, 'well, at least he didn't cost us three important ends by sending our team's winning bowls away from the jack,' and simply answered. 'Well, he did step in at the last minute, and none of us bowled our best. Did we?' Chas noticed the slight curtness in his friend's voice and decided to take a sip of his coffee rather than push the point further.

By now, Roy had already forced two large forkfuls of cake into his mouth and just as the third was being raised to his still half-full mouth, he mumbled. 'So, what did Judith tell you that is so interesting? Was it about me?'

Cliff couldn't resist and replied. 'She did comment that you seemed to be 'putting on a bit of timber', and asked 'is he getting a bald spot?' The fork went straight back down to the plate, and with his right hand now patting his stomach and looking for love handles, his left-hand started hunting, as if it were a police search and rescue operation, for that aforementioned bald spot. 'Stop! Stop! Just kidding,' laughed Cliff. 'She didn't say any of that. You know she likes you. Christ, you're getting vainer than Chas.' Before Chas could comment Cliff continued. 'We don't bowl at the weekend, due to other commitments, but Paddy is a regular here on Saturday mornings, yeah?'

'That's right,' agreed Chas, still stinging a bit from Cliff's comment. 'He helps Marjory Deans with junior training. Apparently he is very good. Patience of a saint, Marjory says, unlike some,' he continued looking directly at Roy who, now happy that he wasn't becoming an 'Uncle Fester' lookalike, was forking the cake into his mouth like there was no tomorrow.

'Anyway, Judith always gets here thirty minutes after the session starts, so that she is ready for the halftime rush. Paddy is normally coaching the beginners on rink 6 while Marjory takes the intermediates on rink 1.'

'Riveting,' muttered Roy, trying not to lose any of his precious cake while he spoke.

Cliff chose to ignore this latest interruption. 'Well, this Saturday, Paddy didn't show and, just like today, without any warning. I think we need to check in on him.' Chas was already one step ahead of Cliff and had got out of his chair. As he made towards the office, he said over his shoulder to the others. 'If he doesn't answer my call I will get his address from the folder in the cupboard.'

Two minutes later, Chas returned shaking his head and with a piece of paper in his hand. 'No reply. Here's his address. Dana and I have to sort out the agenda for our Allotment meeting. Can you two check on him?' Cliff and Roy, who had finally swept up every crumb from the plate, stood up and waved their goodbyes to Judith. She reciprocated by blowing them a kiss. 'That was for me. That was,' beamed Roy. As they left they heard Chas call out to them.

'Keep me in the loop. I'm sure it's just a bad cold.'

....

Cliff drew up outside Paddy's bungalow, which was located only five minutes drive away from the bowls club, he looked across at his passenger and mused. 'Was this guy really a former well-renowned journalist, famous for his insightful and probing reports into the sporting world? Did this guy, through his writing, actually do so much to promote equality within sport?' Cliff found this hard to believe as he watched the ex-Daily Mirror feature writer adjust his seat warmer for the umpteenth time. He had been like Goldilocks. 'It's too hot. Now it's too cold.' Of course, this game had only started after Roy had become bored with the car's SatNav system, 'so you can have all these different types of view: satellite, topological and street view?', and then called Judith at the café to tell her how nice the cake was. 'It costs nothing to pay someone a compliment, about the quality of their product,' he had explained.

'Particularly, when you are after sampling the rest of her goods.' Cliff, of course, kept this comment to himself. He tried not to be annoyed when he saw the cake crumb stained smudges, made by Roy, all over the entertainment consul of his pride and joy, a brand-new Lexus hybrid bought, rather lavishly, to replace his old Audi A3. It had been a sad day for him when the turbo had blown up and Chelsea Steve, his trusty mechanic, had told him through pursed lips that the Audi needed to go to the car graveyard. In this case that meant to the scrapyard next to the dilapidated hotel on the road to Weedon. He had only had the car a few weeks and was still in that hyper-alert phase of worrying about anything scratching or damaging it, but when it came to the interior muck spreader, that was Roy, he determined just to take it to Marty Line, a former car valet at Ford's. When Cliff had been seniors' captain at the golf club he had sorted out a particularly sensitive and complicated issue, involving another member of the section, for Martin. From then on Martin was beholden to Cliff and promised him a monthly car valet as a way of a thank you. With the old Audi Cliff hadn't taken him up on that, but now it was probably time to cash that marker in. Cliff had always been fairly well organised in both his life and at work. This was how he had survived, relatively unscathed, whenever the dreaded Ofsted inspections had occurred. However, his intelligence and skillset did not extend to the practical. Any DIY in the home, beyond painting, was way out his comfort zone. And when it came to washing his cars, he couldn't quite come to grips with the chamois leather, leaving the car smeared rather than gleaming. Consequently, the old Audi had always been taken to the Albanians on London Road. He wasn't going to expose the Lexus to the strong chemicals they used. Not for a while at least.

    Paddy's bungalow was situated at the end of a quiet cul-de-sac in Stefen Hill, well away from the local pub and shops, which were near to where one of Cliff's regular golfing partners, Mack Merlin, lived. Neither Cliff nor Roy had been to this part of Daventry before, and they were both struck by its calmness. Roy said that he had expected to hear the traffic from the bypass, which couldn't have been too far away, but the only sound they could hear at that moment was birdsong. Feeling a sense of inner peace, Cliff led the way, up past Paddy's easily recognisable

Celtic bronze Peugeot, to the front door. It was only as he went beyond the car, and turned to face the door, that Cliff stopped abruptly, holding out his left arm to indicate that Roy should do the same.

'This does not look good,' said Cliff, staring at the front door. Not only was there a paper sticking out of the door, but the lazy paperboy had left another just lying on the step, allowing the elements from the last two days to turn the cover pages, at least, to unreadable mush. Roy walked past Cliff and gathered them up, holding both with an outstretched arm between his thumb and forefinger. 'That stupid paperboy should be sacked,' he commented, separating them. 'Look at this.' He was holding the papers towards Cliff. 'The Observer has been here sticking out of the door since yesterday morning.' Cliff went to the side of the door and rang the bell. At the same time, he put his face against the narrow pane of glass, which framed the left side of the door, craning his neck to allow him to look both along the hallway and down onto the doormat. 'Can't see anything. The connecting door is shut, but there is another newspaper on the floor and some post on top of it.'

'They all must be from Saturday. The postman doesn't deliver until mid afternoon. Bloody Tory cuts,' said Roy, in a scathing voice he reserved for anybody, or anything, right of Keir Starmer. 'Ring the bell again.'

Cliff did so, knowing deep down that the door would have been answered by now, were everything alright. 'I don't like this. Paddy is so well organised. He would have cancelled his papers, if he were going away. Even at short notice.'

'And his car is here. He takes that everywhere,' added Roy.

'Let's check around the back,' suggested Cliff, already turning towards the gate next to the garage. 'Bloody thing is locked,' muttered Cliff, as Roy arrived by his side. 'Go and get the tyre iron out of the boot. It's unlocked.' As Roy was walking back to the car, he heard his friend call out. 'Don't slam the boot.' Roy smiled, knowing that was exactly what he was going to do. Plausible deniability. Cliff snatched the tyre iron from a sniggering Roy and, resisting the desire to clout him over the head with it, dextrously slid it between two panels, adjusting it until he heard a satisfying click. The bolt had disengaged.

'Can't see any curtains twitching,' said Roy, glancing over his shoulder to look at the bungalows opposite. 'Don't want them calling the police. Cliff chose to make a dismissive noise rather than comment and walked into Paddy's back garden.

'Wow, this is beautiful,' opined Roy, as he accelerated to catch Cliff up. Cliff couldn't argue with that. The garden was of a good size with both the lawns and hedges beautifully coiffured. Instead of planting in the borders, Paddy had opted for the simpler and safer route of using a vast array of pots for his bedding plants. Had Chas been with them, he would have bored them by identifying every single one, both by its common name and its Latin one. All Cliff could attest to was that there were plenty of them, in a multitude of colours and all looking healthy.

They walked past the wooden structure, which unobtrusively housed the recycling bins, and found themselves coming towards the conservatory door. At first Cliff thought he was looking at some discarded slippers, but then he realised that they were attached to some bare hairy legs. His pace increased until he stopped at one of the windows. Laying there, on the carpeted floor, was Paddy. His bathrobe was wide open, with its knotted sash performing no more of a job than to cover his belly button. Were it not for the fact that Paddy was wearing some black boxers, his modesty would not have been covered. Fearing the worst, Cliff stepped to the adjacent window. Paddy's head was tilted to the side so that he was directly looking at where Cliff was now standing. Although his eyes were open, Cliff could tell that both the eyes and Paddy himself were lifeless. His mouth looked contorted, giving his face a look of horror, or maybe, surprise. To the side of his forehead was a dark stain, contrasting violently against the light grey carpet. Cliff's gaze was then alerted to a shock of colour. About two feet from Paddy was one of his Aero Quantum bowling balls, bright yellow in colour, as it always had been. This time it looked different. It had a blob of colour on it. The same colour as that of the stain.

Cliff and Roy looked at each other, eyes unblinking. Neither of them wanted to speak, nor to acknowledge what they were witnessing. What could be said anyway? Finally, Cliff took out his mobile phone and hit the speed dial button to connect him with his daughter, Samantha.

Chapter 2

Cliff remained seated at the island situated in the centre of his well-appointed modern kitchen. He never stopped being thankful for the good luck that had afforded him the opportunity to live in such a fantastic house. His eyes followed his good friend, as he, coffee mug in hand, walked out the kitchen door towards his new temporary dwelling, the annexe used by the previous owners as a source of extra income. Roy looked even more hunched than usual due to the events of that morning, and his 5' 7" frame seemed to have shrunk by at least two of those inches. Meticulously dressed, as always in his bowls outfit, he seemed to have lost the spring in his step with his slim legs appearing almost to bow at the knees. Cliff, having always struggled with his weight, envied Roy his more athletic appearance. It wasn't as if it were down to Roy being more of a sportsman in his youth, just a result of genetic chance. To offset the slight belly brought on by time, nature had given the aging Roy the whitest of hair, and to hide the hint of a second chin, the ever-resourceful Roy had cultivated a neat goatee. Although he had his back to him, Cliff knew that Roy's normally piercing blue eyes, even more sparkly when in conversation with a pretty lady, were now glazed and red from the tears that he and Cliff had finally succumbed to after finding poor Paddy lying dead and alone in his house.

Cliff glanced at the large clock to the side of the kitchen door. Was it really only 3.30 in the afternoon? That meant it had been a mere three hours since they had forced their way into Paddy's garden. So much seemed to have been crammed into that time. So much that they would never forget. It had almost been like a release valve when, as waiting for the kettle to boil back in his house, he had phoned Chas and updated him as promised.

Cliff was quite pleased that he had had the presence of mind to phone his daughter Samantha. In spite of the fact that he hadn't been in the same house as her when she was a teenager and maybe needed him most, he had always tried to not let the divorce get in the way of their relationship. It had been difficult at times, particularly at the start when her mother, Julia, had been so confused and angry with the circumstances which had led to them separating. But Cliff had persevered, and their relationship had strengthened when Samantha left her mother's home and joined the police force. A further contributing factor to their improved father-daughter relationship was when Julia had found 'a real man' and moved with the aforementioned hunk of testosterone to Bournemouth. Samantha, as she grew older had, unlike her mother, finally understood her father's reasons for breaking up the family. He had needed to be true to himself and fair to Julia at the same time. After all, not all bisexuals come out of the closet. Statistically there are a lot of women, who are either habitually cheated on, or find themselves mysteriously in a sexually frustrated state.

Samantha had been surprised to receive the call from her father. He knew not to call her at work, and they weren't due to meet for their weekly lunch until her day off, on Wednesday. Upon hearing what her father was telling her, she had immediately, as is standard procedure, alerted the ambulance service, although it seemed too late, and informed her DS, Shelley Wilde. Shelley, at 29 years of age, was two years younger than Samantha, but had been promoted quickly as part of the graduate fast track program.

Sam, who herself became a detective after ten years in the force, knew Shelley to be a good and shrewd police officer, and had no problem taking orders from her. As per her phone call, Cliff and Roy remained exactly where they were. It was possible that any more movement could corrupt a potential crime scene. Cliff had begrudgingly agreed to do so but looking up at the perpetual moody clouds in the sky he added, 'I hope it doesn't bloody tip down as we haven't got any coats on'.

They heard sirens in the distance and the ambulance arrived first, but then saw no sign of further activity. 'I expect they've been told to stay away from the house until the police get here.' Cliff volunteered to Roy. The sound of further sirens filled the air and then there was a bang. Through the conservatory window they then saw two police officers enter the room, placing what looked like small plastic sheets down for them to then tread on. As they stood to the side they beckoned a paramedic to enter. It became obvious that her role was to ascertain whether Paddy was alive or dead. Her speedy departure finally shattered any lingering hope that Cliff and Roy may have had. With their hearts on the floor, Cliff heard his daughter say. 'Dad, are you alright?' Cliff turned and smiled weakly but the shake of his head pulled at Samantha's heart strings. 'I can't get involved at this point, because you are my father. DS Shelley Wilde and PC James are going to take your statements. It's just routine. We always need to take witness statements, particularly when a death is unexpected.'

Cliff and Roy then found themselves being separated. Shelley Wilde took Cliff to the gazebo in the corner of the garden and Roy found himself sitting in a patrol car in front of the house with PC James.

Afterwards, when back in the car and driving to Cliff's house, Roy sounded perturbed. 'I don't know about you, but I felt I was being questioned almost as a suspect rather than as a member of the public, who had just found an acquaintance dead in his house.' Cliff was about to comment when Roy added. 'Bloody big brother tactics. Suspect and oppress everyone. No wonder so many fear the police.' Cliff's blood pressure rose for a minute, seeing this as a personal attack on his daughter, but thought it better to offer a more balanced response. 'I think it makes sense for them to separate us. Different people see different things. I'm certain your PC was just trying to cover all the bases. I think I got lucky being with Shelley. I know her a bit through Samantha, and she was very sensitive in her questioning technique.' Roy, who hadn't really been listening to his friend, just grunted. He had got it off his chest, and now his thoughts were again with Paddy.

Back alone in the kitchen, Cliff stared around and noticed that the normally full rack of coffee mugs seemed almost empty. He got up and went over to the dishwasher, a gadget almost more important than a TV in Cliff's eyes as he loathed washing up. It was empty, not even a spoon. He then remembered he had used it the previous evening, and before bowls had put everything back in its ordered place. The image of Roy disappearing out through the door, with a mug in his hand, flashed into Cliff's mind. 'The lazy git,' he thought. 'That's where they've been going.' He made a mental note to go and retrieve all of his mugs, so that the dishwasher could once again work its magic prior to Chas and Dana popping round after the allotment committee meeting.

Chapter 3

'Look at him,' Chas said, looking over towards the café area where Roy was leaning in towards his server Judith. He was clearly speaking quietly not wanting his overtures to be heard. Judith was also leaning forward towards the aging Lothario, so that their heads were less than two feet apart. She was obviously enjoying his attention, smiling from time to time and even emitting a coquettish giggle, which seemed to spur him on even more. 'If he put as much effort and practice into his bowls, particularly as our lead, then the bloody 'Gerry Hattricks' wouldn't be sitting over there looking so smug.' His gaze had now alighted on their conquerors, who sitting at the same table as the league leaders, 'the Wickies', were taking great delight in sharing every detail of that morning's victory, the second time they had beaten them in a few weeks. This time it was a catch-up game from the previous month.

'Yes,' replied Cliff, whose mind was on something else, something more serious than a massive loss to a normally inferior team, 'but I think none of us played anywhere near our best. It just stands out when, after the lead has played, that we are already two or three down.' In Cliff's mind these forensic post-match dissections, normally negative, served no useful purpose.

'Look,' continued Chas, undeterred, 'Those are our coffees there, and they are getting cold again. A bloody Frappuccino may be ok in the summer, but not at this time of the year.' He pushed his chair back, stood up, and set off towards the café bar. 'Oi, Romeo we want our drinks today.'

'Right, that's enough!' said Cliff, sounding really hacked off. 'Will you two let it rest. No, Roy it isn't unfair that Jerry Naismith uses that 'contraption'. It doesn't give him any advantage. In fact, it requires extra special timing, and it's bloody amazing that he can play at all. We should count ourselves as flaming lucky we have our health.' Cliff had allowed his two friends to continue to bicker, when they had finally returned with the lukewarm drinks, but his patience had finally snapped.

'Maybe, given the way you bowled, you should try using one too,' smirked Chas, always wanting to get the last word in. Roy easily riled by his longtime friend, in fact they could argue about anything if they both were of that mind, opened his mouth to respond, but was cut short. 'We need to talk about Paddy. There I've said it.' Cliff's tone had taken a really serious tone.

'To be honest', replied Chas, 'it's a topic I've been avoiding.'

'Me too,' added Roy, now no longer staring frustrated at Jerry's bowling aid. 'Has it really been two weeks since we found the poor guy?'

'In a way it still hasn't sunk in,' said Chas. 'Because I wasn't there with you, thank God, I've lived in a state of denial, half expecting him to walk through that door at any moment.' He was almost needlessly pointing at the inner security door.

'Same here,' agreed Roy. 'I miss the old bugger. He could always bring a smile to your face, even got one out of old Mick Wartherton once. He should be canonised for that.' The other two nodded, reflecting on the wonderfully positive nature of their lost friend. Mick was a county bowler and fantastic golfer too, but was renowned for his short temper. He didn't suffer fools gladly. Paddy had been one of the only members Mick would go out of his way to talk to.

'Have the police got very far? Chas asked Cliff, knowing that he would be badgering his daughter, Samantha, for details and updates.

'No, and that's what is worrying me,' said Cliff in a tone which drew the others in. 'Because of undermanning……'

'Thanks to those bastard Tories.' Roy couldn't help but to express his contempt of the current Government, but immediately shut up when Cliff shot him the sternest of looks.

'Because of undermanning,' Cliff continued, staring at Roy, almost daring him to interrupt again, 'Sam has been removed from that particular case, but has continued to keep an eye on the investigation, knowing Paddy was our friend.'

'Good girl, your Sam.' Chas was the one to stop Cliff's flow this time.

'What has she told you?' asked Roy, wanting to hear more.

'Apparently the conservatory door was open. Of course, once we saw the body, and that he was clearly dead, we didn't even think to try it.' Roy nodded, recalling the scene vividly. 'They are working on the assumption that it was an opportunistic robbery that poor Paddy somehow interrupted. When I say they I mean Detective Inspector Jeremy Bridges.'

'Paying for that piece of bad luck with his life,' continued Chas, following the logical flow of the police's supposition. 'I suppose it makes sense. The robber probably panicked and struck him with the bowling ball, which was at hand.'

'That's much more than bad luck, if that's the case,' Roy chimed in. 'Have the police got any suspects?'

'According to Sam, they've interviewed all the likely lads. All the local scumbags and scrotes. They all seem to have an alibi, and even those without an alibi can't be placed anywhere in the vicinity.'

'So, two weeks in and they've got nowhere really. Paddy deserves more than that.' There was a resigned disappointment in the way Chas expressed himself.

'Very true,' agreed Cliff, 'but I take issue with Jeremy.' They all knew Jeremy as the current Vice Captain at Staverton Park. The course where they were all members.

'How so,' asked Roy.

'Well for one thing, I remember seeing his car keys on the table in the conservatory. That car is worth over twenty thousand pounds. Surely an opportunistic thief wouldn't pass up that opportunity.'

'Maybe the bastard had a car, so couldn't risk leaving it there. Not after committing murder.' Roy sat back in his chair pleased with his logic.

'Also, stealing a car would leave an evidence trail. Too risky in these circumstances,' Chas added.

'I will give you that,' ceded Cliff, 'but we all know how cautious Paddy was, almost obsessive. I remember him telling me that, after a break in where he used to live, he had a nighttime security routine, checking doors, windows and the alarm. It sounded like a pilot pre takeoff routine.'

'You're right,' said Chas, agreeing with his friend. 'I remember seeing him here in the car park, going back to his car three times to check it was locked.'

'Yes, I saw him do that too,' said Cliff. 'I had forgotten all about it. In fact I think he bought his latest car, primarily because it has folding wing mirrors to show the car is locked.'

'If the police have got it wrong, what can we do…' Roy's question never finished as he suddenly became aware of a pair of 36C breasts leaning across him.

'What are you guys talking about? Judith enquired, clearing the table. 'You all looked very serious.

'So would you if you had played as badly as we did,' joked Cliff. He stood up, expecting his lodger to do the same. Typically, Roy waited until the breasts disappeared from his vision. As he got to his feet his head swayed gently from side to side in time with the rhythm of Judith's seemingly hypnotic posterior. 'In answer to your incomplete question, my horny friend, I'm not sure what we can do at the moment, but we can't do nothing.'

Chapter 4

Staverton Park Golf Club isn't, much to the chagrin of the guys seated in its Clubhouse on that Tuesday morning, a 'members' club. That's to say the club is owned, and run, by the adjacent hotel and not by its members. This being the case the annual £1,000+ cost, depending on whether you wanted to play midweek only or on any day of the week, just afforded the players unlimited golf according to their chosen type of membership.

There were only about ten elderly gentlemen left chatting idly or drinking a lukewarm cup of coffee from the 'extortionate' coffee machine. 'Two quid!' One of them would always exclaim. 'I bought my first car for that.' They were reluctant to return home prematurely knowing that their wives, should they still be on this mortal coil, would drag them down the shops or, even worse, make them do some unnecessary decorating. Some sensible souls, who weren't as desperate as others to get away from their domestic circumstances, had looked out of their windows, checked with 'gorgeous' Carole on BBC Breakfast and phoned in to make their apologies. Thirty others had donned their waterproofs, normally grey or black, and, making sure they didn't forget their umbrellas, set off to the club, more in hope than expectation. Sadly, that expectation was soon shot down when Cole, the head green keeper, had shut the course. Knowing the resentment he would be confronted by, he had taken pictures at dawn, detailing the flooded greens, bunkers and fairways, and on top of that there were stark images of uprooted trees and branches scattered haphazardly around the course. Hurricane Isidro had been seen coming over the past few days and it had left poor old Staverton Park in a terrible state.

Cliff, Chas and Roy were all due to play that day, but unlike at the bowls club they normally didn't play together. Cliff had just said farewell to his regular Saturday four ball partner, Mack Merlin, when he gestured for the others to come over to a table next to the window in the corner of the bar. 'Has nobody told Mack that he looks like Jimmy Saville in that blue waterproof suit? I keep expecting him to light up a cigar,' said Roy, taking his place to the right of his friend.

'Only every time he puts it on,' smirked Cliff. 'That outfit is Galvin Green and cost over £300. No way will he stop wearing it just because of a little ribbing.'

'Look at them,' said Chas, sitting down opposite Cliff. He nodded towards a table where four other men were seated, leaning forward and talking in hushed tones. 'The Quango are up to their tricks again.' Cliff smiled. Like Chas, he disliked the way that certain members of the Committee ganged up to drive through their ideas. It was certainly divisive, allowing the few to make self-benefitting decisions, which would affect everyone, but trying to get new blood onto the Committee was like finding hen's teeth. Cliff, Chas and Roy had all been the whole way along the Committee conveyor belt and now were off the other end, feeling quite despondent by the current situation.

'Forget them,' said Cliff. 'We will find out soon enough what they are concocting.' He looked at them each in turn before adding. 'I think we may have a way to help get Paddy some justice.' He sat back, waiting for this statement to be absorbed.

'How?' Chas didn't look as enthusiastic as Cliff had anticipated. 'If the police can't get anywhere, how can the three of us do what they can't?'

'Because we care, and we have a whole lot of life skills between us.' Chas nodded his head, but still didn't look convinced. Cliff knew how Chas liked to be praised and played that card early.

'My 'how?' is a little different.' Roy spoke slowly, allowing him to compose the question correctly. 'How will we get anywhere near the case? We have no rights of access. We know very little about Paddy. Apart from he was a good bowler and a nice guy.'

Cliff held up a set of keys. 'This is how we gain access to the case, well his house anyway. And that, my dear Roy, is hopefully how we will learn more about Paddy.'

'You have his house keys?' Chas couldn't have sounded more dumbfounded. 'Again I have to ask 'How?'

Cliff took his time before he answered, knowing that he had their interest piqued. 'Well, after our humiliating loss yesterday…..'

'We didn't lose,' interrupted Roy. 'We were robbed by that illegal bowling contraption they used.'

'Oh do shut up!' Chas groaned. 'Firstly, it isn't illegal and secondly, you bowled with the touch and feel of a rhinoceros.'

Sensing this was going off at a tangent like a runaway train, Cliff decided to speak over them, just like he used to do to get 9C Spanish back on track on a rainy afternoon. 'As I was saying, because for some reason my fridge seems to be rather bare,' as he said this he stared pointedly at his lodger Roy, who had his own fridge in the annex, 'I had to go to Waitrose for a restock, and I bumped into Murray.' Murray Ferryman was the incredibly popular leader of their Monday triples team. 'Anyway, we had this rather interesting conversation next to the fresh fish counter.' Cliff paused, looking at each in turn. One of his strengths was to tell a story well. That was why he had so many friends and, as a teacher, had had far fewer problems with poor discipline. 'Turns out that Murray was Paddy's solicitor, and his tragic death had also caused Murray a rather large professional conundrum. Chas, now totally engrossed in the story, wanted to ask 'How?' again, but chose to use another monosyllabic interrogative. 'Why?'

'Because,' continued Cliff, 'poor old Paddy, despite Murray's constant urging, never left a Will and died intestate.'

'That's not normally too big of a problem,' countered Chas, who thought himself to be rather informed on legal matters. 'I'm certain Murray uses an investigator to solve such problems. All he, or she,' Chas was always careful to make sure he was as PC as possible, 'needs to do is look at the records in Somerset House. Or look at past censuses.'

'But therein lies the rub,' smiled Cliff, conspiratorially. 'Murray's investigator has just retired to the Algarve. As a favour he ran some quick online checks, but he could find no evidence of any living relatives. Even more frustrating for Murray, there seems to be no record of Paddy existing prior to him moving to Daventry ten years ago. Murray doesn't feel he can ask the guy in Portugal to do any more'

'Wow!' Roy said, equally intrigued as Chas. 'That must have Murray pulling his hair out. I know he hates the Government benefitting from people's deaths. I feel the bloody same. Bloody parasites the Tories are. People should be given the tools…'

'Get off your high horse,' Chas cut in. 'Is Murray looking for a new investigator?'

'That's the plan, but apparently good ones are hard to find. In the meantime,' Cliff held up the keys again, 'Murray's given us the gig.' Cliff sat back in his chair, rather embarrassed by his use of a much younger vernacular.

Chapter 5

Cliff parked his Lexus in front of Paddy's drive. For an instant, common sense left him as an irrational hope that he'd see Paddy peering out of his front window of the bungalow went through his mind. That thought soon disappeared as the constant bickering between Chas and Roy grew ever louder, bringing him back to reality.

'I still don't know why I had to sit in the back seat,' whined Roy, for what seemed the twentieth time.

'Because I called shotgun,' smirked Chas, 'and with your gamy knee, you had no chance of getting to the car first. If you're a good boy I might let you ride up front when we go back to pick up my car.'

Cliff could hear no more and, pointedly, got out of the car, before shutting the driver's door as loudly as he could bring himself to, without actually slamming it. His rather stilted action, however, still had the desired effect, and as he slowly walked up towards the bungalow, he heard the sound of two other doors quietly shutting.

'Nice street,' commented Chas.

'Of course, you haven't been here before have you,' replied Roy, who was scratching one side of his white goatee beard with his index finger.

'No, first time,' said Chas. 'We have some friends, who used be in the Kilsby allotment society, but for some unfathomable reason chose to move to the other side of Stefen Hill, near the shops.' Chas was a bit of a village snob, but he did stop short at totally belittling anyone who lived in Daventry itself.

'Well Kilsby isn't exactly brimming with action, is it?' muttered Roy, sensing an opportunity to wind up Chas once more.

'I'm glad they've taken down the police tape,' interrupted Cliff, considering what a difficult job NATO did. 'It must have just happened first thing this morning, because when Murray and I came here yesterday to check the door keys worked, you couldn't move for blue tape saying "Crime scene, do not cross".'

That stark and chilling image worked, and Chas and Roy followed Cliff up past the Peugeot to the front door. As Cliff rummaged around in his coat pocket, he nodded towards the car and said. 'When we find the keys to that, we will need to give it a once over as well.'

Although it was only drizzling and they hadn't got their clothes wet, they were pleased to find that the central heating had been left on. They took off their coats and placed them on the near empty coat stand to the side of the door. Cliff looked around but couldn't see any sign of the post and newspapers, which had been by, or in, the door two weeks earlier. He surmised that they had been taken away by the crime scene officers, just in case they might provide some useful evidence.

'Well what's the plan?' Roy asked.

Cliff looked along the hallway, seeing five doors. 'Okay, let's first get the lay of the land. We won't go into any of the rooms yet.'

Being quite a small bungalow, they soon found themselves back at the front door, having done a clockwise route.

'I've heard of an upside-down house,' commented Chas, 'but this is back-to-front living.'

'Makes sense to me,' countered Roy. 'Have the two bedrooms at the front. After all this is a very quiet and small cul-de-sac. And then have the living space overlooking the attractive garden.'

'Yes,' added Cliff. 'The conservatory gives that little bit of extra needed living space, and the little patio affords the garden multi-functionality too.'

'Bloody hell!' laughed Roy. 'We sound like blooming estate agents. Too much time watching flipping "Homes Under The Hammer".' Roy had that knack of summarising anything, but always with a humorous twist. The other two soon found themselves chuckling as well.

Glad for that lighthearted moment, Cliff went on to formulate their plan of attack. 'I will look in the master bedroom and en-suite, while Roy searches the guest bedroom and the living room.' Cliff looked at Roy, as he gave further clarification. 'I doubt the guest bedroom will reveal much, but we all know how much crap we can secrete in a living room.' He turned to Chas, who was awaiting his instructions. 'Roy and I talked about this before we picked you up, Chas. Can you look in the conservatory? You didn't see the body in there, and I think the memory is still too fresh in our minds to concentrate properly.' Chas nodded, as Cliff continued. 'If anyone finds the keys to the car, can they quickly search that to?'

'What about the kitchen diner? I'm happy to do that too,' offered Chas. Cliff agreed, happy that the guys were now getting at least a little focused.

'Remember as well as looking in the glovebox and the console next to the driver, there can be little drawers at the bottom of the front seats.' Chas and Roy looked at each other as if Cliff had gone mad. 'I know,' continued Cliff. 'When I went to Bilbao by ferry to see my friend, Javier, the customs officer pointed out these little drawers right behind where your calves would be.'

Chas and Roy were now grinning. In giving them this piece of information, Cliff had also alluded to one of his many 'online friends'. Although they are an open secret amongst Cliff's nearest and dearest, he rarely brought them up in conversation. Nor did he bring them to the bowls or the golf club. That is apart from Klaus, who played in Staverton's Invitational just before the pandemic. Much to the annoyance of some of the older and less forgiving members of the club, the trophy not only went to Bavaria to be displayed as a 'war trophy', according to ex-Brigadier George 'Bulldog' Drummond, but it remained there through every lockdown of the COVID era, until Klaus came back to win it again in 2022. By this time, however, a new rule had been pushed through the Committee, mainly at the instigation of Bulldog, whereby no trophy now could leave the clubhouse. To Cliff's pleasure, his name, and that of Klaus, now sits proudly on the honour's board. What was doubly funny was that nobody checked Klaus' claim to have been a Colonel in the Bundeswehr. So, every day Bulldog had to put up with the ignominy of seeing Oberst Klaus Von Richthofen on the board right next to 'his seat'. This last piece was actually true by happenstance as the German Golfing union also has to follow the handicap rules of golf.

'Ok, you've given us our places to search,' said Roy, 'but what are we looking for?'

'Anything that can give us a clue as to who Paddy was,' Cliff replied. 'Just gather up anything you think might help us to learn more about him. If you're not sure, add that to the pile. Once finished we can all reconvene in the living room.'

Chas nodded. 'Agreed. It's amazing what information you can glean from someone's pocket or wallet. God knows what we'd find in yours, Roy.' And with that he pretended to shudder and winced, like he had just smelt something awful.

'Come on. Let's get to it,' chided Cliff. 'God it's just like herding cats,' he thought to himself.

....

An hour later, they were together again in the sitting room. Roy and Cliff had positioned themselves at separate ends of the light brown leather sofa, while across the coffee table sat Chas on a recliner, but set in the upright position. This wasn't a time to relax. Chas, who after two recent cataract operations much to his disgust now had to use reading glasses, started the review. 'Well, you'd think a house would give up much more than that about its owner,' he said, pulling the hated spectacles down on his nose so he could see the other two more clearly. 'All I found were his credit cards and his passport.' He leant forward to hold them up, as if giving evidence in a court of law. 'And I will tell you something,' he added. 'He didn't want them found. They were really well hidden at the back of a drawer in the sideboard, underneath a piece of plywood which was similar in colour to the rest of the drawer.'

Roy took his turn pointing to a bowls trophy. 'I almost missed this,' he shared conspiratorially.

'Missed it?' Chas said, bemused. 'There are about fifteen of them over there in that cabinet.' He pointed to the one thing in the whole of the bungalow, which could be described as slightly cluttered. And that was because there were so many trophies.

'Yes,' smiled Roy, enjoying his moment, 'but the others are all recent. This one is from the last century. And what's more,' he paused, enjoying being the centre of attention, 'it's from Derry. Last time I looked at an atlas, that's in Northern Ireland.'

'Wow! That is intriguing,' commented Cliff. 'Did anyone find his phone?' Chas and Roy shook their heads. 'Me neither,' he went on, 'but I did find this.' He held up an iPad Pro. 'Not sure what use it will be without Paddy's password, but it still could be useful.'

'So that's it?' Roy commented.

'Not everything,' Chas replied. 'Sorry, I forgot. I found his car keys and had a quick look. No joy.'

'Even in the secret drawers?' Cliff asked.

'Even in the secret drawers,' laughed Chas. 'But I remember seeing in a TV crime drama that the SatNav records its data. It could tell us where he has been. Might be useful.'

'Certainly could,' agreed Cliff. 'Old Billy Malloy at the bowls has a son who is an electrical mechanic. Always useful to know such people.'

Roy looked around the room. 'It's so sparse,' he said. 'A monk would have more personal belongings. Is there anything else we have learnt, do you think?'

'His wardrobe is neatly ordered,' offered Cliff. 'There's a place for everything and everything is in its place, is the phrase that comes to mind.'

'Sounds military,' suggested Chas.

'Yes, you're right. His black dress-shoes are so shiny you could almost shave using them.'

'I'd never have pegged him as a military man,' commented Roy.

'Me neither,' agreed Chas. 'He seemed too funny and popular to have been in the forces,' he added, thinking of the tartar that is Bulldog.

'Actually,' said Roy, who was scanning the bookshelves, 'as well as some guidebooks, there are a few war history books and the odd Andy McNab and Chris Ryan novel.'

'There were a couple more of those on his bedside table,' said Cliff. 'I will tell you something else. This is the only house I have ever been in with so few photos. Apart from those three of him, and his partners, at the awards night.'

'It's like he has no family, at all,' said Chas.

'Or doesn't want to be reminded of them,' commented Roy. 'I've got four wives I would rather forget,' he added with a smile.

'But not the kids Roy,' said Cliff. 'You love them surely?'

'Most of them, I suppose,' laughed Roy.

'Right,' said Cliff, standing, 'I think we've done everything we can here.' He started to carefully put their discoveries into the large Adidas hold-all he used for his regular short trips away. He smiled, remembering a few of the items he had removed earlier. He knew the ribbing he would take if these two, Roy in particular, ever saw them. But they added to the overall enjoyment of such liaisons, and Joe, the 65-year-old widower in Teignmouth from last week, had already asked Cliff back for a repeat visit.

'We will meet at mine tomorrow morning at 10 o'clock. I know Chas has to prepare for the annual Garden Society quiz night, and I am on duty at the Samaritans.' Chas and Roy both knew that it wasn't really the Samaritans, but he was on call once a week at the LGBTQ+ switchboard. He had done this throughout COVID, because of the ability to be able to do so from home. Afterwards, he had tried to give up, but his life skills and personality had made him so valuable to the switchboard that he had been persuaded to stay on. He didn't ever deny his sexuality, but also chose not to broadcast it. Hence, the using of the Samaritans as a cover. In a sense it was true, just more client specific.

Roy was leading their small group out of the living room when he suddenly stopped. This meant that Chas, who because he was turning to talk to Cliff, walked right into him.

'What the hell!' Chas stopped his tirade as he followed Roy's line of vision.

'There's a loft,' pointed Roy. 'Didn't even think of that in a bloody bungalow.'

Cliff pushed past and looked up at the ceiling. 'How did we miss that? There must be a way up there.' Chas was already in the kitchen. In the space between the fridge and the wall, he had earlier noticed a broom with a hook on its handle. At the time, he hadn't thought any more of it, but now it made sense. He walked back to the hallway, holding it in front of him like a flag-bearer at the Olympics. Unfortunately, his prowess at getting the hook into the right position, so as to pull the hatch open, was less impressive.

'For God's sake, give it to me,' said Cliff, who with great dexterity quickly pulled the hatch open to reveal a folded ladder attached to it. The hook once again proved useful and soon they were watching Chas, because the battery on his phone was the only one with enough charge to use the torch app for any amount of time, climb up into the loft. Roy had, despite his physical shortcomings, offered to go in his stead, but Chas shot that proposal down saying, 'do you think I'm letting you touch my iPhone 14 pro?'

It turned out that the loft was empty, save one small rucksack, which contained two rather surprising items: a silver military medal and a Diego Maradona Argentinian football shirt.

'These must be special or significant. Heaven knows why,' said Cliff. 'Right let's get out of here. We can come back if we need to. Murray has left the keys in my safe keeping and there is no immediate time limit.'

Chapter 6

When Cliff first moved to Daventry, he went there with his then wife Julia and their three-year-old toddler, Samantha. He was only in his fourth year of teaching and had just been promoted to 2nd in the Modern Foreign Languages Department at Southbrook School. Julia had previously given up work as a PA almost as soon as her maternity leave had ended and didn't have any inclination to go back. 'A young child needs its mother', she would say by way of justification. This meant that money was tight. Although people often bemoan the amount of holidays a teacher gets, they rarely look at the pay in terms of being an adequate living wage. Particularly, in a situation such as Cliff's. At the interview he had seen some warning signs as to the nature of behaviour issues in the school, but the lure of an extra £1,500 for his new middle-management role, together with a slightly cheaper housing market, caused Cliff to overlook his concerns. Even with the access to relatively more affordable housing, Cliff and Julia could only extend their expenses to an ex-council house on Heman's Road. Being no more than a two-up two-down, it was still an upgrade to their small flat in Hemel Hempstead.

For two years, Cliff fought the demons within. At work, the job was thankless. Daventry, lying almost slap bang in the middle of the country, was a town on its way down. Shops and businesses were closing and being replaced by the ubiquitous 'Pound shops' or branches of the many local charities, such as Air Ambulance. Because many of the more academic and hard-working pupils sought a grammar school education over the border in Warwickshire, leaving Cliff to try and inspire those that remained. And that was a daily attritional battle. Cliff thought it much akin to that at Stalingrad. Arguments such as "Why do we have to learn a language, they all speak English?", "I'm never going abroad, anyway" or the more brutal "It's boring" were heard on a daily basis. Somehow, through the support of many good colleagues, who comforted one another in the sanctuary of the staffroom during the morning breaks and lunchtime recesses, Cliff hung on to his sanity. It was indeed a difficult school in which to teach, with terrible behavioural issues and below average examination results. It even had a MLD, Moderate Learning Department, for the real nutters. To illustrate the nature of the Southbrook pupil, this was managed not by a qualified teacher but by an ex-prison guard. Cliff was actually a very effective teacher, who got more out of these pupils than anyone else in the Department by in his words 'entertaining more than coercing'. For that reason, when his Head of Department was signed off on mental health grounds the day after they were told that Ofsted were coming in, he had to take over. As a result he was rewarded with a further £1,000 per year for running the Department permanently. To be fair, it was just recompense as he helped the rest of the Department to get only one 'poor' assessment and he himself got an outstanding grade for both of his observations. The school sighed collectively with relief when it learnt of its overall judgement, 'Satisfactory'. Cliff, on the other hand, decided then and there that he'd retire as soon as possible.

That resolution had one large major obstacle, finance. Cliff should never have married Julia. It was a mixture of peer pressure and a genuine hope that his true homosexual preferences would somehow disappear. He did his best to live up to his manly responsibilities as a husband in the bedroom, and for a few years he succeeded. It was never true lust but a combination of youthful pent-up energy, and a vivid imagination, usually replacing Julia in his mind's eye with some guy off one of her favourite soap operas. The quick arrival of Samantha helped in this area. Julia was often 'too tired' and Cliff used that excuse as well, with Cliff eventually claiming that the stress of work had brought on premature impotence. He hated himself for this and eventually told Julia the real reason. Initially, because of the venom of her reaction, he regretted his decision but he knew it would end up being for the best. She went to her parent's house that very evening and from that night on they never spent another day in the same house, let alone bed. Her father, being a solicitor, saw to it that Cliff was hung out to dry. She got the house in the divorce settlement and he was ordered to pay the maximum alimony possible. Cliff couldn't afford to rent even the cheapest of properties, but salvation came in the form of his Deputy Head, Simon Swilson a recent widower, who offered him a room for as long as he needed. Cliff could finally be true to himself and, almost more importantly, to his family.

Cliff, under severe financial restraint, continued to work at Southbrook. He tried to find a job in a school with a better cohort, but once you teach at a school such as his, where there are no 'A' level classes, he found himself labelled as not having proven teaching experience with higher ability pupils. What he could do, however, thanks to Simon's generous, almost non-existent, rental expectations was to work flat out during the weekday evenings, ensuring by end of school Friday he was prepared for the following week. This gave him ample opportunity to pursue his new lifestyle. This usually meant getting the train from Long Buckby to Birmingham on a Saturday, and from there going to the Gay Village where he would frequent the saunas, bars and clubs until the small hours. Sometimes, he would get lucky and find himself waking in the arms of another man. Other nights, he would stay in one of the various 24-hour institutions, to save money, and then get the milk train home.

Although Cliff was embracing gay life, he wasn't really into the scene. If truth be told he wasn't attracted to younger men, nor was he keen on the extreme promiscuity he saw from some. This was the time of the AIDS epidemic, and he wasn't willing to play Russian roulette with his life. He was fundamentally on the hunt for a partner, someone to share his life with. After a few years of this lifestyle, Cliff was beginning to feel that 'safe' one-night stands were his only hope for intimacy, but then he met Doug in a quiet cocktail bar and his life changed.

Doug was ten years older and, unbelievably, a Hartlepool United fan, who had organised a local book signing to coincide with his team playing at Solihull Moors. As he had travelled there alone he decided to go to the Gay Village afterwards. Cliff and Doug hit it off immediately, with Doug inviting Cliff back to his hotel. In Doug, Cliff had found a soulmate, and one that fitted in perfectly with their very different schedules. Once a month, Cliff would go to Hartlepool and stay in Doug's large Victorian house. The others he could now devote to building bridges with his daughter. By this time, Julia had remarried, Tony a builder, so both her attitude towards him and alimony demands had calmed quite a bit. Staying on as Simon's lodger, more out of friendship than requirement, put Cliff on a much more secure financial footing and this afforded him the opportunity to take Samantha on at least two foreign holidays a year. The rest of his holidays Doug made himself available and they lived as a couple. For many years, this blissful lifestyle continued. It even made Southbrook bearable. However, all good dreams, just like nightmares, come to an end, and one very cold January, Doug caught pneumonia, passing away a few days later. Fortunately, Doug's niece, Jayne, knew of their relationship and contacted Cliff. Simon approved Cliff's compassionate leave and he got to Hartlepool in time to see the love of his life one last time. Cliff had never felt so bereft in his life before and took diazepam for a month, trying to come to terms with this traumatic experience. All his life, Cliff had battled the demons caused by homosexuality and now finally they had started to overpower him. In this time of extreme darkness, Doug once again brought light and hope to Cliff. Apart from bequeathing his house to Jayne in his will, everything else, including future royalties, went to his 'partner' Cliff. The net value of Doug's estate was £3.7 million. Cliff knew that Doug's Headland series of murder mysteries were popular, but didn't realise that crime writing could be so lucrative. It took a while for Cliff to appreciate the magnitude of this gesture, but once he did, Cliff quit his job and, with Simon's approval, bought the large house next door, which was for sale. It seemed as if it were written in the stars. There was one star in particular, which Cliff often noticed because of its special twinkle. One that reminded him of the way Doug used to look at him. Whatever its real name is, to Cliff that is Doug watching over him.

Cliff still lived in that house on Ashby Road, but unfortunately Simon had succumbed to the pandemic. It often brought Cliff to tears thinking of poor Simon dying alone in that hospital, with nobody allowed to be with him in his final hours. He was having one of those moments when he heard the doorbell. It was Chas, punctual as always. He rang Roy to tell him to come over and reflected that he was doing for Roy the same as Simon had done for him. That seemed right somehow. Friends helping each other in trouble, but in his case Simon had just been a kind acquaintance, before becoming so much more.

Chas and Roy were already bickering over something inconsequential when Cliff brought in their coffee and biscuits.

'Glad you haven't skimped on the biscuits,' said Roy, picking up two chocolate-chip cookies to dunk in his coffee. 'At Chas', you are lucky to get a plain digestive.'

'Don't go there Chas,' smiled Cliff, sitting down in his favourite armchair. 'We all know you and Dana are generous hosts.'

'Well at least we actually buy our own coffee and don't surreptitiously nick some from our friend and host.' Chas couldn't resist getting one little dig in.

Roy's face reddened and his mouth opened. For once no words came out.

'Don't worry Roy,' said Cliff, 'I know all about it. Have you not noticed the motion sensor security cameras all around the house?'

Roy's face was now crimson. Cliff knew that he was now worrying about what else the cameras had revealed.

'Right, before we look at the stuff we found at Paddy's, I need to let you know about an email Sam sent me late last night.'

'An email?' Roy looked confused. 'Why would Sam email you? We aren't too old for WhatsApp and texts.'

'Because, 'he who walks around my kitchen butt naked at night', she was sending me some documents.' Cliff enjoyed throwing in that embarrassing titbit. 'Some documents we might find useful, but she could get into big trouble for doing this. So mum's the word.'

'Of course we won't say anything,' said Chas. 'What sort of documents?'

'Details from the autopsy report, replied Cliff. 'Physical things which might help us find out who Paddy is, I mean was.'

'Bloody hell, she has taken a risk there. I know you are her dad, but this is major,' commented Roy.

'I think she has more faith in us than she does in that twat Jeremy Bridges. How did he ever become an Inspector?'

'I know,' agreed Roy. 'I wouldn't think he could detect a fart in a lift.'

'Now that is a beautiful image,' said Chas, shaking his head at the crassness of his friend. 'What does the autopsy tell us?'

'Firstly, his body had experienced a lot of previous trauma. He had scars on his torso, one which could have been caused by a knife or a bottle, and another that looked like a bullet wound. He also had two historical bone breaks. One in each leg, femur in one and tibia in the other.'

'I suppose you never can tell what lies underneath a bowling shirt?' Roy mused.

'Well, if he were a golfer he might have had the required post match shower where that could have been noticed,' added Chas. 'As a bowler we don't ever shower in the club. Not exactly a sweaty sport. Was there anything else?'

'Death, as we know, was from a blow to the head, but what is more interesting it that there are two concentric blows. The first is thinner and seen as tentative, probably made by a hammer or crowbar. As they are still working on the assumption of an opportunistic burglary, they think this might be from one of the tools of the trade, so to speak.'

'Makes sense,' commented Roy, 'but why two? What do they say about that?'

'The second must be from his bowl,' interjected Chas.

'Quite right,' continued Cliff. 'They think it was done to try to mask the first blow and make it look like manslaughter.'

'How so?' Roy was struggling to keep up.

'Because if the murder weapon was brought along to the house by the killer, then it would be deemed to be premeditated.' Chas rewarded his smartness with a swig of coffee. The others watched with smiles on their faces, waiting to see his facial expression change when he realised it was stone cold. They weren't disappointed.

'That's true,' said Cliff, getting back to the topic in hand, 'and Sam reckons that a lesser pathologist might have missed it. Apparently it takes a force of 250 kilos to crush a skull as it did with poor Paddy.'

'Yes,' said Chas, 'that killer was clever. Doubt a pock-faced teenager could have come up with that plan.'

'Correct,' agreed Cliff. 'There are two more visual clues, tattoos. The first is XX and XY.'

'When you said XX,' interrupted Roy, who is nowhere near as stupid as he looks, 'I thought roman numerals. There is no Y in roman numerals, so I think they might be his children. Aren't they the chromosome descriptions for male and female? Or something like that.'

'You're right,' said Chas. 'What was the other tattoo?'

'Now that one is weird,' answered Cliff. 'An alphanumerical tattoo, totalling a random mix of twenty one numbers and letters. Let me make some more coffee. We have to look at the contents from Paddy's house and formulate a plan.'

'Don't forget to bring some more cookies.' Roy held up his empty plate and smiled.

Chapter 7

Cliff sat there nursing his empty cup of coffee, reflecting on the meeting, which had just finished. He glanced out of the window just in time to see Chas' silver Kia Sportage turn out of his drive, onto the Ashby Road. It would take him about ten minutes to get home, providing the traffic lights for the perennial roadworks on the A361 weren't set to red. Cliff smiled, at his friend's choice of car. Just like Chas, it wasn't showy, and brilliantly represented his character, trustworthy and dependable with an enviable strength of character and a power to get the job done. He knew that when Chas got home he would be going straight into his study, probably with a coffee and slice of Dana's Victoria sponge, to research the medal.

Cliff had total trust in Chas to do the job thoroughly and effectively. What had surprised him earlier was the focus he had seen on Roy's face when they were discussing their investigation. He knew Roy had been a very successful and renowned Sports reporter, but in his mind he had dismissed him as just that, a sports reporter. He tended to think of Roy as a match reviewer, forgetting that in his pomp he had won awards for championing equal pay for women in tennis and uncovering a gambling ring based around the Pakistan cricket team. The search for justice for Paddy seemed to have regenerated a spark in Roy and he had volunteered to research the bowls trophy. He said he had a contact who he thought would be an asset to their enquiries, and with that he had left Chas and Cliff in the sitting room, setting off for his annex. Even more surprising, he hadn't finished his latest pile of cookies.

The other clues or potential routes of investigation were left to Cliff. He was going to get Billy Malloy to look at Paddy's car SatNav. At that point he wasn't sure of all his next steps, but he was determined to get access to the iPad Pro. He was going to hold on to the passport and credit cards. Maybe Sam could help with accessing Paddy's bank account, but that might be asking too much. Finally, he was going to go to a local tattoo artist to see if there was a way to find out anything about the strange nature of Paddy's body art.

....

Chas had used the time it took for his laptop to boot up to polish off a second slice of cake. He felt it was his husbandly responsibility to quality check the standard of Dana's baking. After all, the upcoming Kilsby produce fair was approaching and Dana didn't want to lose to Cynthia James. Again. Everyone has a nemesis, and even the wonderful Dana, who saw their friend Cliff's well-being as her responsibility, is included in that statistic. You only had to mention Cynthia's name to see a cold look go across Dana's face.

'Well?' Dana enquired, as Chas loaded the side plate into the dishwasher.

'Really tasty,' he replied. 'Obviously, using my homemade raspberry jam gives it a unique flavour.' He smiled, looking at his petite wife, now favouring an auburn version of the Judi Dench short hairstyle. 'Of course, if you win that should mean I get named as well.' He narrowly dodged the tea towel aimed at his backside, which disappointingly was slightly larger than it used to be. Chas considered this a badge of honour, reflecting the diligence of his quality checking.

'I thought you had an investigation to get on with,' she laughed, turning back towards the oven. 'I've got to be careful not to burn my scones. Now shoo!'

Back in his neatly ordered study, Chas opened the contacts folder in Outlook. He had customised it with background notes on most of the addressees. This helped him to personalise any email. He scrolled down until he found the name, Albert Bloomsbury. Bertie to anyone who knew him. In his notes he had written "former colonel in the parachute regiment, but unlike most former officers he doesn't like to use his rank. Send cards etc. to Mr. A Bloomsbury". Chas sat back and thought for a while before picking up the phone and dialling.

'Bertie? It's Chas from the allotment society. I have a conundrum and could do with your expertise.' Having outlined the situation, they had opted for Plan B. Plan A was for Bertie to come over and look at the medal and then for them to research together online. They both concluded that this probably wouldn't provide them with all the answers they needed. Plan B was for Chas to pick Bertie up the following morning, and for them to go by train to the Imperial War Museum in London. As soon as he ended the call, he opened the Trainline app on his phone and booked them cheap day return tickets. Anyone who knew Chas wouldn't have expected anything else. He would treat Bertie to his day in London, after all he was giving both time and help, but he drew the line at buying first class tickets. When he was a town planner and then a councillor, people would often be heard mimicking his favourite phrase. 'How much?'

....

Roy was glad that his former colleague at the Daily Mirror, Sinead Murphy, hadn't changed her mobile phone number, because she no longer lived in Kilburn as he had thought. It turned out that the former political editor had returned, a few years previously, to Belfast to care for her elderly mother. His affair with Sinead had been the reason behind divorce number two. Apparently, his then wife didn't care 'to share him with some provincial trollop!' The affair hadn't lasted, and Roy soon moved onto wife number three. One of the things that had attracted him to Sinead was her northern Irish burr, so it made his stomach turn over, in a nice way, when she answered the phone. She had worked in Derry during the troubles when she worked as a cub reporter for the Belfast Telegraph. As she shared caring responsibilities for her mother with her younger sister, she suggested that Roy fly to Belfast, and that they would then drive in her car to Derry. Roy was slightly disappointed when she said if he were on the first flight out, then he would be able to return on the last one back.

'No last hurrah in a hotel, then,' he sighed, as he found availability on the next day's flights.

…………..

Cliff had fallen asleep in his chair, only to be woken twice, once by Chas' phone update, and then Roy roughly shaking his shoulder so that he could organise a lift to Birmingham airport the following day. 'And I will need picking up too,' said Roy, going off to pack his cabin bag. Cliff gathered himself, feeling pleased with the progress already made by the other two, but at the same time was also a little disappointed with his lack of momentum.

He knew Billy Malloy would be home by then, so he called and organised to meet Billy at Paddy's bungalow the following morning after dropping Roy off at the airport. He then contacted Sam, who flatly refused to 'use police resources to check on Paddy's account. That is a sackable offence, even if you are working for his solicitor.' She also agreed that going through the proper channels would be slow and hung up in red tape. Feeling a bit despondent, Cliff was thinking about the iPad, when he saw that he had received a text from Sam. It simply gave a number and address, stating, 'this might be your way in.' Cliff went straight onto Google maps and saw that it was the address of a computer repair shop in Weedon. Five minutes later, he had booked an appointment for the following afternoon.

He sat back in his chair and, with a contented smile, shut his eyes once more. 'Looks like we are all having a busy day tomorrow,' he thought. He hadn't remembered about the tattoos, but had he looked a bit closer at Google maps, he'd have seen a tattoo shop was two doors down from his appointment in Weedon.

Chapter 8

Chas picked up Bertie, as arranged, from his house in the nearby village of Barby, and drove them to the car park adjacent to the railway station in Long Buckby. As pleasant as the fifteen-minute drive had been, because Chas always found Bertie to be engaging company, the shock at the cost of the daily rate for parking a car there turned his smile upside down. Had he been with Dana, he would have turned around and sought the nearest free parking space irrespective of it meaning a ten-minute walk, but with Bertie alongside, he decided to bite the bullet and pay.

Long Buckby is a much smaller station than the neighbouring ones in Rugby or Northampton, and that meant it was on the slow train line, stopping at every station en route to Euston. Chas calculated that the saving he had made by not using the quicker Virgin trains from the other stations, had almost offset the extortionate fees for parking. This made him a little more content with life as he settled himself into his reserved seat opposite his friend.

'Show me the medal then,' asked Bertie.

'Not much point,' replied Chas, reaching for a box in his inside jacket pocket. 'Unless you know the ribbon colours by heart? All the medal has on it is the Queen's head and the usual Latin phrase or two.'

Bertie smiled, taking the box from Chas. Chas could see him opening it, putting his hand inside, but couldn't see anything else. 'It's a Falkland's service medal,' he smiled, looking incredibly pleased with himself.

Chas looked at him incredulously, and gasped. 'Leave it out Bertie, you can't be sure. There must be hundreds of ribbon colours on our military medals.'

'You are right. There are, and I certainly can't name many medals by their ribbons.' With that he held up the medal, having removed it from the box. 'What I can do, even with these tired old peepers,' he continued turning the medal around, 'is read.' He leant forward towards Chas, so that he too could see the writing on the reverse side of the medal. Sure enough, under the ribbon, nicely striped in a blue-white-lime-white-blue mirrored pattern, he read the words 'South Atlantic Medal'.

'We didn't think of taking the medal out to check what was on the other side,' he said, face palming and simultaneously laughing out loud. 'The guys are going to be as embarrassed as I am.'

'No harm done,' consoled Bertie. 'That's a good starting point though, giving us a reference campaign with dates to focus on. By the end of the day, we should know a lot more.'

The rest of the journey was taken with Bertie telling Chas about his own medals. Chas, always a good listener, was enthralled by Bertie's stories and the rest of the journey flew by.

At Euston they made their way straight to the underground lines. The Imperial War Museum is located on Lambeth Road, which meant their end station for this trip was Lambeth North, on the Bakerloo line. Having had to change tubes once, they finally emerged back at ground level on Lambeth road.

'That may be the most efficient way to get around London, but I bloody hate the underground,' said Chas, pulling at his shirt, which even in the coldness of winter had started to stick to his body.

Bertie, who annoyingly looked as cool as a cucumber, agreed. 'Yes, the noise and ventilation could certainly be better, but as you say it is quick and easy.'

They emerged from the tube station and back into the winter chill. A brisk walk of less than ten minutes along Kennington Road meant that they soon found themselves passing the huge double-cannon, which stand sentry in front of the entrance to the museum. On the tube Bertie had explained that he had had to pull a few strings and get special dispensation to get them on that day's appointment list. 'Had to call in a few favours'. It turned out that the research room, which is located on the second floor, has to be pre-booked, allowing only fifteen individual researchers per day. On top of that, each researcher is only allowed to request up to ten items per day. 'That's for Johnny Civilian,' said Bertie, tapping his nose with his forefinger. 'If you have the right clearance and clout from your military time, they will bend over backwards to help you.' Chas smiled inwardly. He had certainly made the right decision in getting Bertie on the case.

As they had arrived thirty minutes before their appointed time, they made their way to the IWM North café located on the ground floor. While Chas stood in line waiting to buy them both a coffee and snack, he looked around at the well-appointed spacious refectory. He was glad he had sent Bertie to sit down, because he wouldn't have been able to resist comparing it to his idea of a typical NAAFI, and he certainly didn't want his ignorance to upset his friend. Instead of Wagamama style communal tables with wooden benches running along them, this café was decorated in a far more relaxed style, full of small intimate tables and soft furnishings. As for the drink, the menu was varied and fairly priced served in either china cups, or for more added realism, bully tins made from tin-plate. The food was no longer only of a long-life variety, as would have been needed for campaigns in the past, but fresh with lots of healthy options.

As he sat down, placing their coffees and jam scones, served the Devonshire way, in front of their seats, he noticed that Bertie was studying the medal.

'I thought so,' said Bertie. 'I couldn't be sure in the train, and certainly not in the underground, but here in the more natural light without the constant bouncing movement, I can see that I was right.' Chas waited for this to be developed, but Bertie looked as if he had finished. Instead of continuing he kept focusing on the rim of the medal.

'You can't leave it at that,' said Chas, more than a little exasperated.

'Oh, sorry,' replied Bertie, realising his mistake. 'It's the rim you see. Normally, they have the military social security number of its recipient engraved there.'

Chas missed the key word 'normally' in that statement and smiled, thinking that their job would soon be solved. However, Bertie's next words soon had that smile wiped from Chas' face. 'Unfortunately, my fears were well-founded. Whoever your guy was, he certainly didn't want people to know anything about him.' With that, he thrust the medal towards Chas, who had been just about to bite into the jam covered scone in celebration. Having carefully placed the scone back onto its small plate, he took the coin and put on his reading glasses. Screwing his eyes as if it would help make the numbers reappear, he swore silently.

'If you ask me,' said Bertie, 'I think it was done in a bit of a rush. You can still feel the outline of some of the impressions. With the help of a magnifying glass, we might be able to work out some of them.' Chas felt along the rim and understood what Bertie was advocating.

'We know Service numbers go in a 123-45-6789 pattern,' continued Bertie. 'So if we have another medal to look at, to compare the size and location of the number, we should be able to create a Blankety Blank version, which should help with our search.'

Chas nodded, and took an optimistic bite from his scone.

The Imperial War Museum is spread out over six floors, but they didn't need to go beyond the second floor, where the research room is located. In all of the films Chas had seen, where people were researching old records they always seem to have to use microfiches. As he surveyed the well-lit large room, he could see a lot of computers, in fact sixteen of them, each allocated to an individual research table or the curator's desk. But there were no micro fiches. As they were being taken to their table, he asked the curator about them.

'Well, we do have some in a neighbouring room, but during lockdown we took the opportunity to start transferring our older records to our existing digital system. We have used interns and other available staff to continue that ever since,' he explained. 'If your search is pre-1914, then you will have to use the older technology. As Colonel Bloomsbury indicated the approximate age of the serviceman you are researching, I don't think you need to trouble yourself in this case. This should be the only tool you should require.' He pointed at the PC on the desk. 'If you find what you need is located in a library book, then my job is to bring it to you. There is no need to login. The system is ready to use.'

With that he started to turn, but was stopped in his tracks when Bertie called out.

'We need a magnifying glass to help us start. Do you have one?'

The curator leant behind the computer screen and produced a large magnifying glass on a stand. Chas calculated that it was approximately seventy percent the size of the computer screen itself. 'Is there anything else you need to get underway?'

'Yes,' replied Chas, 'If we only have a partial Military Social Security Number, is there a database search tool which could help?'

The curator, who until then had looked a little bored, smiled, and sat down on the chair. His knowledge of the software was impressive and in less than a minute he stood back up. 'You can see that box on the left side of the screen.' He didn't pause thinking it self-explanatory. 'Well, that is formatted to the nine-digit system we use. If you know the number, then type it in. If not put an "x". It's as easy as that.'

The guys thanked him, and immediately set out to find an image of another South Falklands Service Medal online. Using the very efficient magnifying glass, they finally agreed on four numbers, with another one being a possible. Chas, being forever cautious, suggested they go with the four they were confident of. He filled in the box, using an x where there weren't sure. Finally, he asked Bertie to check his work and then hit 'enter'.

'773 records found!' Chas' voice was full of dismay. 'We can't check all those. It will take days.' He slumped in the chair, and turned to look at Bertie. Instead of seeing Bertie's face next to his, he saw Bertie heading off towards the curator. Thirty seconds later, the curator was back in the chair.

'Of course, we can narrow it down,' he comforted. 'Firstly, it's a man.' With that he checked another box. 'Then we know his approximate age, so we can narrow that down, too.' They agreed a rather generous service range, and the curator, whose name they now knew was Fred, entered those figures. This time, the search revealed thirty-six records.'

'Now that is much better,' commented Bertie. 'Thanks Fred, we can work with that.'

Two painstaking hours later, they had whittled it down to four candidates, who had all served in the Falklands, and whose service photo bore a resemblance to Paddy Cullen.

'How do we know which one he is?' Bertie was starting to show a little frustration. So near yet so far. 'What else do we know about him?'

'Well, he was Irish. If not, he did a bloody good impression,' replied Chas. 'Where do these guys come from? Do they have any links to Ireland, or maybe Scotland? A lot of people can get those confused.'

Bertie looked at the hard copies they had printed of the four possibilities, and then said. 'Two are cockneys, well southern anyway. One is from Cornwall. So that leaves....' He passed the record to Chas. The more Chas looked, the more Paddy started to appear.

'That's him,' he said, excitedly. 'I'm sure of it. That's him. Best be certain though.' He took out his phone and took a photo of the soldier. He then sent it to Cliff and Roy on their bowls team's WhatsApp group.

Replies soon returned. Firstly, from Cliff. 'That's him. Well done.' Then from Roy. 'Chas mate, good work. You've found him.'

Chas showed Bertie the messages and they smiled at one another.

'Now what do we know about this bugger,' said Bertie, looking once again at the file.

'So, Paddy Cullen was really James Paisley,' observed Chas.

'Yes, and you can see why his accent was so convincing,' replied Bertie. 'Born in Ayr on November 5th 1951, but of Northern Irish decent.' Bertie paused. 'Yes, thought so. From a Protestant family.'

'Looks like he joined the Army straight after leaving school in 1970.'

'Yes, initially he was in the Royal Scots regiment, now the Royal Regiment of Scotland, and was promoted quite quickly to the rank of corporal. Served a stint in Cyprus, but obviously he was a bit of an adrenaline junkie.'

'How so?' Chas interrupted. Although he was reading the same page as Bertie, he hadn't made that leap at all.

'Look.' Bertie pointed at something on the page. 'In 1975 he went for training in Hereford. That, to me, means one thing. He joined the SAS.'

'Ah, of course.' That made Chas remember a few tedious nights when Dana forced him to watch SAS Rogue Heroes. For somebody not athletically minded, save golf, bowls and gardening, the physical attributes of these elite soldiers made Chas feel very inferior. A lot of the filming had taken place in Herefordshire too. He looked at Paisley's army record below that date and asked. 'Why is so much after that blocked out in black? It's like it has been redacted.'

'Yes,' replied Bertie. 'There are some things the Army, and/or the Government, want to remain secret. Above my pay grade I'm afraid, and I don't think the curator, or anyone else here for that matter, will be able to shed light on that either.'

'So, we are stuck then?' Chas looked more than a little disappointed.

'For the moment, yes,' agreed Bertie, 'but I may have a source who can help me. Let's go home.' Bertie wouldn't elaborate, and Chas didn't want to lose his goodwill by pressing. He comforted himself with the fact they had unmasked the true identity of the man he had known as Paddy Cullen. That was a success for sure.

They thanked Fred for his help, with Bertie pressing a twenty-pound note into his hand as they left. 'You need allies in this world,' he said by way of explanation. At Euston they had 45 minutes to spare so they had a celebratory gin and tonic to go with their paninis. Unsurprisingly, they both fell asleep on the way home.

....

'Chas? It's Bertie. Hope I didn't wake you up, but I thought you'd want to know this ASAP.' Bertie pronounced the acronym as a word. This was probably Bertie's only trait that might make you aware of his military background. It was 11pm and Chas would normally have gone to bed, but he and Dana had become absorbed in a jigsaw, a frustratingly difficult one of a magnolia bush.

'No, Bertie. Good to hear from you.' He said, making his voice sound as positive as the late hour would allow. 'What have you found out?'

'Well, I used to know a guy from the SAS, Lieutenant Colonel Mike Wilkes. It was when I was stationed nearby, in Salisbury.' Chas wanted to hurry him up, but had to be patient. 'Anyway,' continued Bertie, 'me and my former wife, Veronica, palled up with him and his wife to play bridge, of all things. I hate the bloody game, but Georgie his wife, is drop dead gorgeous and made it a lot less boring.'

'Come on, Bertie,' chided Chas. 'A bit of background is good, but I don't need to hear about your sexual fantasies.

'Oops, sorry. Once I was reassigned, I never saw Mike again, but even though we are divorced, Veronica and I are still friends. While we were in the Imperial War Museum, I remembered her telling me that she and Mike started to play online bridge during the lockdown. I wasn't sure whether she was still in contact with him, so I gave her a ring when I got home.'

'And is she?'

'Yes, apparently they were in an online tournament this evening. She said she'd get him to call me, as soon as it was over. That's why I'm calling so late. We've just finished talking.'

Chas continued to listen, taking notes. Bertie had told Mike about Paisley and the redacted records, which seemed to mainly cover the period 1978-1983. According to Mike the earlier part of that timeline might be linked to the troubles in Northern Ireland. The SAS were used quite extensively, and for different clandestine roles at that time. As the medal suggested, he had more than likely been on some secret missions during the Falklands War, maybe to the Argentinian mainland. Chas thanked Bertie, promising to keep him up to speed. With Dana already tucked up in bed, the ever reliable Chas powered up his laptop and typed up his notes. To counter the excitement from the success of the day's chase, he treated himself to a large Brandy. 'Better than a sleeping tablet,' he mused, taking a sip of the golden nectar.

He wouldn't have been so content had he seen Roy's WhatsApp message.

....

Cliff had finally given up, and could listen to Roy babbling on no more. Initially, he had been pleased to see the enthusiasm written across Roy's face. He had been mildly interested in his bowls story from the previous night. Roy had agreed to mark at

Murray's singles match against the very unpopular Mark Church. Any fifty something, who wears a baseball cap, to hide his comb over, and dark glasses indoors in winter is bad enough, but the sheer arrogance of the man irked every single member of the club. Somehow, Mark was blind to the resentment everyone felt towards him. Blindness could explain the dark glasses, but the absence of a retriever and the fact he had been club champion for four years running, soon sent that thought from Cliff's mind.

When he heard that Murray had battled well but narrowly lost, Cliff started to zone out. This was probably a good decision, as he had become bored hearing of Roy's amorous intentions towards the fair Judith. Had he been listening, he would have been reaching for a sick bag when Roy, like a lovesick teenager gushed, 'she wondered whether I fancied a drink sometime, something alcoholic. But as I had already told her of the trip to Derry, the poor girl is going to have to wait a few days for a bit of Roy loving.'

As they approached the entrance to the passenger terminal, Cliff realised that his friend was now on his other favourite topic, LiVARpool. As a Wolves fan, there had been fierce discussion, and even a few days of sulking between them when the ludicrous offside rule had allowed Salah's goal, thereby pushing Wolves further into a stressful relegation battle.

'Well safe trip. Keep us updated,' Cliff said, patting Roy on his shoulder with one hand and handing him his carry-on bag with the other.

'I will mate,' smiled Roy, who had trimmed his goatee that morning just in case Sinead felt a bit frisky. 'I wonder whether you can buy duty free on a flight to Belfast?'

Cliff smiled as he drove towards the exit barrier. 'Five pounds! Just for dropping someone off. What a rip off.' His smile had quickly disappeared, but returned when he mused. 'I'd pay a lot more to evict him though.' He knew he didn't mean it. In fact, he enjoyed having Roy around. It was a fun thought nonetheless.

The flight, as with all internal flights, was shorter than the time Roy had spent in the airport waiting to board. Roy normally would have had an alcoholic drink both before and during the flight, but he realised he needed to have all his faculties for what was to come. Having no luggage to check in, Roy breezed through the arrivals hall carrying his small cabin bag. Cliff had insisted he bring a notebook and pen, but it was Roy himself who decided to bring a change of underwear and a fresh shirt. Just in case, of course.

It had been more than ten years since he had seen Sinead, but he couldn't fail to recognise his former co-worker and lover. Her black hair was slightly shorter now, but her fiery brown eyes and well-proportioned figure hadn't changed at all. Not in his eyes anyway. He was relieved that there was no uncomfortable moment as they embraced. They had been, and were still, at ease with one another, and it certainly didn't upset either of them to be in each other's arms once more. This time it was a lingering embrace rather than a passionate night together.

The small talk that followed as they headed towards the short stay car park gave Roy an idea of where the airport was located. He thought the airport was named after the footballer George Best, but Sinead said that he had flown into Belfast International Airport, which is located quite a way to the west of Belfast near the eastern shores of Lough Neagh. Apparently, George Best is to the east of the Belfast city centre. That meant a shorter and quicker journey to Derry. Once they were on the M2, Sinead searched for cafés nearby on her SatNav. Fifteen minutes later, they were in a small village just off the M2 having a coffee and discussing their plans for the day. Roy showed her the picture of the bowls trophy and retold the story so far. Sinead then used her iPhone to research bowls in Derry. She saw a significance in the location of the only bowls club, but chose not to share that with Roy. She knew nothing about bowls, as a sport, and decided to have no preconceptions. The rest of the journey took less than an hour, and Roy chatted happily away. Small talk, even in bed, had always been natural to them, and so it remained. Roy enthused about the beauty of the country, one he had never been to before, and Sinead was pleased to act as a sort of tour guide. The atmosphere was both relaxed and cheerful. When he asked about the health of her mum, her answer was short and laughter died for a few minutes. Roy quickly changed the topic, giving Sinead a run down on divorce number four.

'You are just the same,' she commented. 'Always thinking the grass is greener. Why can't you just be content and sexually frustrated like the majority of middle-aged married men?' Her accent, even with judgmental tone, stirred something inside him. The truth was that she had been the one, who had got away. Maybe the 'forever' one.

'I think they all end up getting fed up with me, as well,' he replied.

As they entered the outskirts of Derry the tranquility and peacefulness of the beautiful countryside gave way to buildings and reminders of the Troubles. Some were subtle, like a few Union

Jacks to show the area was Protestant. Others were more blatant, like the police station, which looked as if it were built to withstand a nuclear attack. Roy shuddered as he remembered the news clips which almost daily showed stark scenes of unrest and violence.

'Well, here we are then,' said Sinead, as she stopped the car. Roy, who had still been visualising the devastation shown on the News so many years ago, looked out of the window. They were in a car park, and to the right stood the impressive building which the car park served.

'Lisnagelvin bowls club.' Roy read the sign above the door.

'Yes, this is the only bowls club listed for miles,' replied Sinead. 'Come on. Let's go in.' With that, she opened the driver's door and got out. Roy followed Sinead into the club. It looked more like a very upmarket golf club. There was a grandeur and gravitas to the building. There was no reception as such, not in the foyer anyway, but there was a door with the words 'Secretary's Office' in rather large gold leaf. Sinead knocked and, without waiting for a response, entered. Roy followed, happy to let Sinead break the ice.

Five minutes later, they were being given a tour of the club.

'Of course, back in the day you would have had a wasted trip,' explained Ian Donaldson, the silver haired club Secretary, who in Roy's mind, would feel underdressed in a two-piece suit.

'Why is that?' Roy, who had shown Ian the photo in the office, was beginning to feel less like a working class intruder. It was just a bowls club after all.

'Because we only built the indoor section at the turn of the century. So no winter bowling before then.'

'I only bowl indoor,' said Roy. 'Golf all year round. Bowls in the winter.' Roy was obviously trying to bond with Ian to ensure his help, but the rather disinterested way Ian said 'interesting', showed his ploy hadn't really worked. 'Bloody snob,' thought Roy. 'Get on with it then.'

They found themselves walking around the indoor bowling part of the building. On the walls were a mixture of photos and honours boards. By way of clarification, Ian spoke once more. 'We decided to rationalise our system and put these here. We have much more space, and it is there for people to see throughout the year. Now do you have that photo?'

He took the photo, and with amazing technical dexterity for an octogenarian, he picked at the screen to enlarge it. 'Ah, yes,' he said, '1979 men's singles champion. I thought I'd remembered it correctly.' He pointed at the picture in front of him and then to the adjacent honours board. 'I fear you will be disappointed in your quest here.'

Roy and Sinead looked at the name of the winner on the board, Gregory Girvan.

'Could that be Paddy's real name,' thought Roy.

'Look Roy,' said Sinead, staring intently at the picture. 'If that is Mr Girvan, as listed in the picture, then he is seventy years old at least. Much too old to be Paddy.'

'Yes,' confirmed Ian, 'that is Gregory, my uncle and bowling mentor. I think there is one more thing you need to see.' They followed Ian back to the main foyer, until he stopped in front of a massive trophy cabinet. 'As you can see the men's single's trophy is much larger and made of gold. The one in your photo is a silvery colour.'

'I thought this was the only bowls club in the area.' Roy was obviously a little confused.

'It is, and it has always been the only proper club.'

'Proper club?' Sinead was also trying to make sense of this. 'Have there been improper clubs?'

'Yes, in the past,' replied Ian. 'Today we are a mixed club, but sadly back then it was for Protestants only.'

'I take it, by improper, you mean a Catholic one. Was there one of those?' Roy asked, cursing bloody religion in his head.

'For a few years back then, I heard tell of one in Brooke Park.'

Back in the car, Roy exploded. 'What a pompous prick. Sectarian bowls. Bloody hell!'

'Yes, I'm afraid he is,' replied Sinead, a Catholic by birth but atheist by choice. 'Don't suppose you saw the picture of him in his office?' Roy shook his head.

'Decked out in his bowler hat, and the rest of the absurd garb associated with the Orange Order. How the hell is this country ever going to heal when those twats stir things up every summer with their bloody marches?' Roy realised that this wasn't really a question addressed to him, but Sinead venting about that Protestant Order's desire to poke the hornets' nest by insisting on marching near, or even through, staunch Catholic areas.

They drove on, towards the river Foyle. Sinead explained that the area across the bridge would be a Catholic one. Once over the bridge, the town took on a totally different feel. The Union Flags had been replaced by the Irish tricolour, and there were large murals, on the sides of buildings, either celebrating their martyrs or the freedom the Catholics felt that the area gave them. Roy found the massive images both moving, but also a little inflammatory. If Sinead thought the Protestants were at fault for provoking things with their marches, then these murals, even though more benign, were certainly doing something similar. He smiled when he saw a few murals depicting the recent sitcom, Derry Girls. A programme which was set during the troubles, but focussed more on the character and warmth of the normal people rather than the hatred manifested by the paramilitaries. 'Maybe there is hope things will eventually smooth over completely,' he thought.

They parked in a multi-story car park near to Brooke Park. Roy, who had been travelling since dawn, was pleased to be walking in the open air. He resisted the urge to link arms with Sinead by pushing his hands firmly into his overcoat pockets. Although he was happy to be away from the rain in the Midlands, which still meant the golf course was closed, the temperature in Derry was a few degrees less, and Roy hated the cold.

The park was larger than they had imagined and was obviously a well-used and much-loved part of Derry. There was an abundance of facilities, but no sign of the former 'improper' bowls club. Given the topology of the park, Roy surmised that there were only a few spots flat enough. They bought themselves a coffee at a kiosk, using the opportunity to ask the middle-aged woman serving them if she remembered bowls in the park. She had a vague recollection from her childhood of something in the bottom field, but couldn't remember any more. She did point towards a pub across the road from the park saying that it had been family run for generations. 'If anyone does remember it, you will find them in there,' she said. 'On one side of the counter, or the other.'

Glad to be back in some warmth, Roy ordered a whiskey for himself and a slimline tonic for Sinead. He even bought the barman a drink. In his exhaustive research in bars over the years, Roy had learnt that the best way to ingratiate yourself into a new establishment is to get the bar staff onside. Kelly's Bar was overtly in need of some tender loving care, but what it lacked in décor was more than made up for by the friendly atmosphere. Even at lunchtime it was loud and raucous.

The barman, they found out during a rare quiet moment, turned out to be the new landlord, Seamus Kelly. He said he that he didn't remember much about the bowls club. However, he pointed at two men studying the racing pages of The Racing Post in the corner. 'Talk with the cantankerous old git on the right.' He was laughing as he said this. Sinead and Roy looked at the rather podgy, balding man whose stubby fingers was turning the pages, obviously in a quest to select a 'sure thing'. For a man described as cantankerous, he seemed to smile a lot and seemed to have a friendly word for anyone who walked by. 'That's' ma da, Michael,' continued Seamus. 'If that old bastard doesn't know something, then it's not worth knowing.' Roy looked at the old guy again. He looked so comfortable and happy that Roy found himself envying him his look of contentment.

'Da!' Seamus yelled. 'These nice people need your memory. Now try not to bore them.'

Michael's fellow gambler found them two chairs and waited patiently for the interview to finish. Roy supposed that it went with the territory of being Michael's friend. He was obviously used to people demanding Michael's time, and that Michael was too polite to ever say no. The bowls club in Lisnagelvin was viewed during the Troubles as a sign of Protestant supremacy. So much council money, which could, and maybe should, have helped the poorer Catholics to barely survive, was poured instead year after year into that facility so that it became a target for Catholic hate. Had it not been located right next to the well-manned and heavily armed police station, the IRA would have blown it to smithereens. In fact, there were two abortive attempts where Republican soldiers were spotted en-route, and lucky to escape with their lives.

The idea of building their own bowls club was formulated in Kelly's Bar itself. Instead of wasting their resources, which could be safer and more effectively used elsewhere, on the bowls club as a target, it was seen as a monumental v-sign to the Protestants for them to have their own facility. Even if it were slightly rough and ready. They called it the City of Derry Bowls Club and they made sure the Protestants were constantly reminded of its existence. What followed was lots of tit-for-tat news reports, with each side of the divide claiming to have the true champion playing at their club. The UDA became so pissed off that one night in the early 80's the wooden clubhouse was burnt to the ground. That could have been rebuilt, but petrol, or something toxic, was poured over the rather pristine lawn, making it unplayable for years to come. Michael knew a few of the local bowlers but was a darts man, and couldn't really say who the champions were.

'So, if they were taunting one another back then,' mused Sinead, 'then there might be a picture in the local newspaper. Let's go search their archive.'

As they got up to go, Roy received a WhatsApp message from Chas. He opened the picture and yelled. 'He has found him.' He showed the picture to Sinead.

'We haven't got too much time,' she said. 'I will get the car and bring it around here. You show the picture to Michael, and the other older regulars. See if they can put a name to the face.' With that, she swept out of the pub, looking like the old investigative reporter that she had once been.

'He's a bloody squaddie,' exclaimed Michael. 'No way he'd have looked like that. We'd have made him a mile off. Hold on I will get my wife. Women look at men differently you know.' His accompanying wink made Roy laugh. Roy thought he was developing a man crush for this endearing old man.

It took Siobhan, Michael's wife only five seconds to identify him. 'That's Padraig O'Toole. Remember Michael? He was a provo soldier, who lodged at Mary and Brian's around the corner.'

Before Michael could speak, there was an almighty bang. Roy had no idea what was going on, but that sound instantly brought back terrible memories to anyone there, who had experienced the horrific conflict which dominated the latter years of the previous century.

The men ran outside, fearing the worst. Roy followed still not taking in the possible severity of what had just happened. Outside, he followed the gaze of the others towards the multi-storey car park. Initially, all he could see was lots of smoke, and then lower down he could see flames. A panic started to set in, and he counted the floors, beginning with the ground floor. It was the third floor, the floor where they had parked.

His panic turned to pain. 'Oh, no!' Roy yelled, pushing past the throng. 'Sinead! No, no!'

Roy continued his way towards the horrendous scene. He wasn't thinking and certainly, had he stopped to work things through, didn't know what he could do when he got there. He just needed to do something, to reach Sinead. As he started to sidestep people coming the other way, fleeing from the car park, he felt a strong tug at his left shoulder. He impulsively resisted and tried to shrug whoever it was off, to no avail. The person not only held on, but got hold of his other shoulder, pulling Roy backwards. All of a sudden, the helpless Roy found himself in a bear hug, with any resistance on his part proving futile.

'It's me, Seamus from the bar.' The words were spoken strongly, yet with a soothing quality, from an intimate distance into Roy's ear. 'Let's wait here. Help is coming. Look!' As he said that, Seamus used his strength to twist Roy to his left. Sure enough, there was a cavalcade of blue lights and vehicles of all sizes speeding up the road towards them. To his right, Roy sensed the arrival of a second person. It was Michael.

'Seamus is right, Roy,' he said, now standing in front of Roy. 'Let the professionals have space to do what they do well.'

The next twenty minutes were a nightmarish blur. Roy, in a total state of shock, could recognise a sense of continual movement in and out of the building. The smoke had lessened and the flames had disappeared, or burnt out, allowing paramedics to finally be able to follow the firefighters up the stairs, carrying their bulky life-saving equipment.

Throughout this difficult and emotional time the Kellys never left Roy's side. At one time, he heard Seamus admonish someone who had decided to film the scene on their phone, maybe in the hope of earning a little money, or a few extra followers on their social media account. Although the shock of what had happened had robbed Roy of any clarity of thought, he was aware of the silent respect being shown by the resilient people of Derry's Bogside. That lone budding paparazzo apart, people just stood there watching, hoping and praying with crucifixes being kissed and rosary beads being twisted to count their prayers.

A voice in the ether called out. 'Look, they've brought out someone.' Roy, who had been focusing on the third floor, looked down and saw two paramedics carrying a stretcher towards an ambulance. He tried to see if the person on the stretcher was Sinead, or even if the blanket was covering the victim's head, as a sign of respect to the dead. But he couldn't do either.

Michael, who must have slipped away, reappeared next to Roy. 'I've just been talking to the police over there. For Protestants they aren't too bad,' he said without emotion. 'The victim is a woman.' Roy let out a massive groan and slumped. Seamus, who had never left Roy's side, caught him and helped him back to his feet. Michael continued. 'I explained who you are, and because of that they told me she was in a dark blue Volvo.' He waited, while Roy took that in. When Roy nodded, tears now running down his face to confirm the make of Sinead's vehicle, Michael went on. 'She is alive, just. They are taking her to Altnagelvin Hospital. Now you've confirmed that it is your friend, they will allow us to follow. Seamus, get the car. I'll wait here with Roy.'

Seamus finally managed to work his way through the myriad of emergency vehicles, but by that time he must have been ten minutes behind the ambulance at least. Michael had sat in the back with Roy. He knew words were not needed, just a friendly presence. Ignoring the car park, Seamus parked the car right outside the entrance to A&E. Before they had got out of the car, Michael noticed his best friend's son, Declan O'Shaughnessy, now a sergeant in the Police Force of Northern Ireland, coming out of the building. He obviously had been waiting for them. Michael feared the worst. At least the news would come from someone Michael respected. Initially any Catholic police officer was looked down upon and hated, but if the Good Friday Agreement were to work, then there needed to be equality amongst those who enforced the law as well. That equality hadn't yet been achieved, but 32 percent of police officers identified themselves as coming from a Catholic background.

'Roy, is it? I am Sergeant O'Shaughnessy.' Roy nodded. 'I'm afraid your friend, Sinead Murphy, died on the way to the hospital.'

'Oh, no,' gasped Roy. 'Are you sure it's her? Do I need to identify her?'

'We found her driving licence in her purse,' he replied. 'That will do for now. We will need someone from her family to do a formal identification later. If you could confirm that she was wearing a black coat and leather boots, that'd help to give us an informal confirmation for now.'

Roy sobbed a little as he remembered her at the airport, looking immaculate as always, in her black ankle boots and figure-hugging black trench coat. 'Yes, she was,' he confirmed.

Seamus, can you and Michael take Mr .....'

'Grimble,' finished Roy.

'Can you take Mr Grimble to the police station?'

'No problem,' replied Seamus.

Despite his protestations, Seamus and Michael refused to leave Roy's side. Declan had phoned ahead to tell the desk sergeant to allow them to wait in interview room number 1, ensuring that refreshments be also provided. One hour and two cups of coffee later, Declan entered the interview room. Seamus needed to go back to the pub, for the evening session, but Michael stayed with Roy, 'for moral support'.

The experienced policeman let Roy tell his story at his own pace, only interrupting on the odd occasion when a little clarification was needed. He was intrigued by what he heard, and made copious notes.

'So you think Paddy Cullen was known by the people of the Bogside back then as Padraig O'Toole?' Declan asked.

'Yes, according to Michael's wife. She seemed pretty certain,' replied Roy, looking to his newly found friend.

'One of the skills needed by a pub landlady, a great memory for faces,' agreed Michael.

'Surely the explosion isn't linked to that,' said Roy. 'That's over forty years ago.'

'At the moment we can't rule any possibility out. The Scene of Crime Team are working under lights there as we speak.'

Roy glanced at the large clock on the wall. He was going to miss the last flight. Declan saw this look and said. 'I realise you were supposed to be going home tonight. We will sort you out with another flight tomorrow afternoon just in case we need to talk again in the morning.' He smiled and added. 'We can get you a room in the local Premier Inn. I've heard the beds are very comfortable.'

'No need for that,' interjected Michael. 'We have a spare room. My wife would never forgive me if I let Roy spend the night in a strange hotel.'

Twenty minutes later, a grateful Roy was sitting in the saloon bar with a double whiskey on the table in front of him. Apparently, a few police officers had been in just before, asking the older regulars about their recollection of Padraig O'Toole. He picked up his mobile and messaged Cliff and Chas with the sad news.

....

Cliff was relieved that Roy's early departure meant he was driving back on the A45 through Coventry just before the rush hour got fully underway. The myriad of traffic lights and speed cameras made it an onerous journey, if you timed it incorrectly.

Glad to have made it back with time to spare, and without major delay, Cliff parked up outside Paddy's bungalow and waited for Billy Malloy's son to arrive. Almost on time to the second, he saw Billy Junior's Mercedes van turn the corner and stop behind Cliff's car.

Cliff got out of his car and pulled up the collar of his coat to protect himself from the bracing north-easterly wind. 'At least it isn't raining,' he thought. He smiled, as he saw Billy Jr. pour himself out of his vehicle. After shutting the car's door, he adjusted his work overalls, which his large frame filled to excess, making him look like a relative of the Michelin Man, and walked with a bow-legged gait towards Cliff. As he took Billy's outstretched hand, Cliff couldn't help but marvel at Mother Nature, and, in particular, at genetics. If you put Billy and Billy Jr side by side, you would have to be blind not to realise that they are father and son.

'Thanks for coming,' said Cliff. 'Sorry, if I've interrupted your work.'

'Happy to help,' replied Billy. 'Dad always speaks highly of you and this will earn me a few extra Brownie points with him. Me and the wife are wanting to go to London for a show with an overnight in a hotel. Doing this will give me some leverage, when we are negotiating babysitting.'

Cliff led Billy up the drive to Paddy's car. He took a key fob from out of his trouser pocket and opened the door. 'That's as much as I can do,' said Cliff, with a grin. 'Can you access the data on the SatNav and tell me where he has been recently?'

'Is that all you need?' Billy asked, and a relieved look spread across his face. 'That won't take long at all.'

Within moments, he had returned from the van with a toolbox in one hand and a computer case slung over his other shoulder. Cliff watched in awe from the passenger seat as Billy, suddenly defying his bulk, went about his work. Soon he was sitting with his laptop on his knees and nimbly using the touchpad to gain access to the requested data. Cliff could see the laptop's screen suddenly fill with information.

'Think that's everything,' said Billy. 'What's your email address? It's easier if I send you the data as a file.' Cliff reeled off his gmail address, and within ten seconds heard his phone ping, an alert indicating the expected email had already arrived.

'That should be it,' exclaimed Billy, who was now packing everything up. 'If there is anything else you need, let me know. I have a back up, should you delete the file by mistake.'

Cliff thanked Billy profusely and gave him £100 in cash. 'Hope you and your wife enjoy the show. This should get you a nice meal, even in London.'

....

Cliff arrived outside the computer repair shop in Weedon feeling a little unhappy. He had forgotten that Staverton Golf Club would shut its clubhouse whenever the course was closed for any reason. As many of the holes were still flooded, the staffing resources had been diverted to the main hotel, and Cliff found the doors to the clubhouse locked and the lights off. Not having time before his scheduled appointment to go home, he had to make do with a 'meal deal' from a garage. Cliff looked at the crusts of the half-eaten egg and cress sandwich, which had its stale ends pointing to the sky, and the garishly coloured empty bag of cheesy Wotsits and thought, 'not exactly deal of the century.'

Cliff carried the iPad Pro into the shop, almost dropping it as the security door signalled his arrival with a decibel level akin to that of an air raid siren. Cliff was expecting a pock-faced computer nerd to be working there, but behind the counter stood a middle-aged man wearing an open-necked shirt and a light-grey two-piece suit.

'How can I help you?' The man had an educated accent, certainly no hint of a local twang. Cliff held out the device and explained his predicament. The man listened closely, but shook his head as Cliff finished. 'Sorry. We can't unlock devices for just anybody.' Cliff fished around in his inside pocket and brought out a letter from Murray's law firm.

'Phone them,' he said. 'They will tell you that I'm on the up and up.'

The man returned from the back-office, still looking uncomfortable with the state of play. 'My daughter, Sam is a police detective. She will vouch for me too.'

'Sam Doyle?' He asked. 'Why didn't you say that before? She was brilliant when we were broken into last year.'

Feeling rather smug, Cliff shut the door to his car and placed the piece of paper containing the iPad's six digit password next to the bag of Wotsits. He looked at the mess and decided, instead, to fold it into his wallet.

As he looked along the street for a bin, he was dumbfounded to see a Tattoo shop three doors down. 'Serendipity,' thought Cliff, gathering up the remnants of his disgusting lunch, and getting out of the car once more.

Relieved that this door made no more of a sound than a gentle chime, Cliff turned to see a woman with short cropped black hair wearing a black singlet. He did his best not to look shocked as he saw that, apart from her face, there was not a square centimetre of her skin, which was not covered in ink of one colour or another.

She, in turn, looked Cliff up and down and asked. 'What can I do for you love? We do have some older people requesting to have their name and address tattooed on their forearms.' Cliff's bemused look showed he required further explanation. 'Dementia you see,' she smiled.

'What if they think it's the name of their loved one? They'd all be worried they were gay,' laughed Cliff.

'Hadn't thought that through, had I.' She was laughing along with Cliff. 'Seriously, what do you want? We don't often get senior citizens. It's the wrinkles you see.'

Cliff took out his phone and showed her the photos of Paddy's tattoos. 'What do you make of these?'

The woman took the phone from him and looked at the two photos. Cliff was fixated by the tattoos on her long slender fingers. Each one looking like it depicted a card from a tarot pack.

'Not much to go on,' she commented, studying them closely. 'This one, the XX and XY. Very amateurish. Not quite prison amateur, but had a boyfriend once who was in the forces. That quality was about the same. Obviously depicts a boy and a girl, probably his kids. Secretive not to put their names though. But this one,' she was looking at the alpha-numerical tattoo, 'is more professional. The definition is top notch and the ink quality is up there too. That one is built to last.'

'Any ideas?' Cliff asked, in hope more than expectation.

'Normally it's a code or password for something. Hardly ever done anything like that myself. Are you sure you don't fancy a tattoo?'

Cliff, who had often toyed with the idea of having a tattoo of the Wolverhampton Wanderers FC logo, reluctantly shook his head. He hated needles. He thanked her for her help, and set off for home.

....

The dishwasher in the kitchen was loaded and a full glass of Malbec was resting on a coaster to the left of Cliff's recliner chair. He had rewarded himself for a very fruitful day by ordering a takeaway curry, lamb tikka pathia, onion bhajis, pilau rice with a peshwari naan. It had only taken two mouthfuls to forget the abomination that had been the egg and cress sandwich. Having drunk tap water with the meal, he relished the first sip of Malbec, allowing the rich, deep flavours to move from one taste bud to the next.

He needed to prepare a report for the others, so he picked up his notebook and began to make notes, not in a linear form from top to bottom, but with bullet points coming out of each oval heading. He wrote the first heading "SatNav", and then drew the oval around it. He had already read the file sent by Billy Jr., but needed to reread them once more before he started to scribble. Once he had finished, he checked the statements for both brevity and accuracy. Apparently, Paddy must have known the local area quite well as there were no destinations in Daventry. He had searched for a few car parks in the local towns of Rugby and Northampton, but apart from that his other searches had been for bowling clubs in Northamptonshire, or neighbouring counties, and two airport terminals, namely Birmingham and Heathrow, terminal 5. Cliff knew that Paddy had relished playing inter-club matches, so it wasn't a surprise to see these as destinations. Knowing that Chas would expect it, he made a list of the clubs in alphabetical order. That act afforded him another sip of Malbec. He then highlighted the airports to remind himself to cross-reference them with the passport and the calendar on the iPad Pro.

Not wanting to dull his brain, he decided to put his next sip of wine on hold, and opened Paddy's passport. Cliff wondered how, if this wasn't his real identity, Paddy had secured what looked, to all intents and purposes, to be a genuine document. He filed that thought for later, and opened it at the identity page. He could see that seven of its ten year life had passed, and that it therefore wasn't due for renewal until 2026. The photo of Paddy was pale and stark, with Paddy staring expressionlessly at the camera. Cliff's passport was about the same age and he certainly looked, in his photo, like he had aged much more than Paddy in the interim. 'Bastard,' he thought, and took an involuntary swig of his wine to assuage his sudden melancholic feeling about getting old. Since Brexit had changed so many things, there was now a stamp from the Spanish immigration at Valencia, dated February that year. Cliff remembered that Paddy used to go there regularly for winter sun and because of that was a member of an ex-pats outdoor bowling club near the beach. He had been going there, and to other Spanish clubs, for as long as Cliff had known him, but his earlier visits hadn't needed him to get entry and exit stamps. Cliff could hear Roy now. 'Bloody Brexit! What selfish, brainless twats voted for that? Can't see any new freedoms, but I can see a fucking mountain of red tape and hassle.' He wasn't going to discount the importance of Paddy's regular trips to Spain from their investigation, but there were other entries, which piqued his interest more. Numerous stamps showed that he had visited Switzerland quite regularly, normally Zurich, but once he had been to Geneva. That didn't appear too strange to Cliff as he knew Paddy enjoyed hiking, but the appearance of Buenos Aries in three stamps was something he hadn't expected.

Fixated by the trips to Argentina, Cliff remembered the Maradona shirt found in the loft, but couldn't progress that line of thought any further. He decided to use the password and unlock the IPad Pro. The first thing he did was to check the emails, but they were all but empty. Either the bowls club was the only source of his emails, or he routinely deep-cleaned the inbox, along with all the other boxes, such as "trash" and "spam". He went onto Safari and, once again, the history there was empty. Cliff hardly ever did this, and blushed at the thought of people seeing his search history. Actually the people searching would blush even more. He saw a NatWest banking app, but knew that would also be encrypted. He would need all of Paddy's fingers and both of his retinas to gain access.

As the glass was between him and his mobile, he took another small swig before dialling Murray's mobile number. The call finished just as Cliff polished off the wine, and he looked at his notes. Murray as Paddy's solicitor had access to his bank account and the information he had passed on was beyond strange. Paddy had no work's pension, nor did he have a state pension, despite being well over the official retirement age of 65. What his account did show was regular deposits of cash into his account. These deposits were frequent and very large, always five figure sums. Cliff reflected on this for a while and then a thought hit him. He went back onto Safari and did a quick search. 'That's it,' he thought. On the screen in front of him, he could read. "International Bank Numbers (IBAN) are twenty-one alphanumerical characters long", just like the tattoo. 'You have a Swiss bank account you old bugger.' Cliff was speaking to the screen. 'How and why would you have one of those?'

Before he could pursue that line of thought, he heard the familiar whistle of his WhatsApp notification. It was Roy telling him of what had happened to Sinead, and that he wouldn't need to be picked up from the airport until tomorrow.

'Bloody hell! What have we gotten ourselves into?' he was speaking to the ether this time. As he didn't have to worry about drink driving, he poured himself another glass of Malbec and sat back into his chair.

....

Seamus had left his wife Kathleen to run the bar, and, as agreed, picked up Michael and Roy from the police station's car park to head towards Belfast International Airport. Declan had almost insisted on Roy receiving a police escort instead. Initial forensic reports had shown that the explosion hadn't been accidental, but the result of a bomb. What made Declan concerned for Roy's safety was that it wasn't just any old bomb, but a home-made explosive known as 'Anfo', a fertiliser and diesel oil mix, favoured by the IRA when they had been at their most active. The police investigation into Sinead showed her, as a Catholic, to have no clear links to terrorism, and therefore there was no reason for her to be targeted in such a way. As there hadn't been a bombing in over twenty years in Derry that left them with the strong possibility of Roy being the target, with his investigation into Padraig O'Toole being the root cause. As such, Declan felt he needed to share as much as possible with Roy. He felt duty bound to impart the little he had discovered about the mysterious man known in the Bogside as O'Toole.

A terrorist database search had certainly located him, but details were scarce. He was listed as a soldier in the Provisional IRA and his address was as Michael's wife, Siobhan, had remembered, but that was almost the full extent of his file. There was nothing about him before his time in Derry, and he seemed to disappear again after 1980. Although, the database on members of the terrorist group often was incomplete, this file was suspiciously light.

Michael and Seamus went with Roy right up to the departure gate. Roy, normally not given to emotional outbursts, particularly with other men, shook Seamus' hand, thanking him profusely, and hugged Michael, almost not wanting to let him go. He promised to call them when he got home. Cliff, back in England, was primed to pick his old friend and lodger up at Birmingham.

Chapter 9

Chas returned from the Kitchen, carrying a tray of coffees. Of course, as they were dining chez Dana, that meant a small bowl complete with tongs of Demerara sugar cubes and an accompanying milk jug, full fat being the only option. For different reasons, Cliff and Roy had both tried to turn down the invitation to dinner that evening. Cliff wanted to contact one of his admirers in Argentina. Due to the time difference, he knew he needed to do it before 10 p.m., while Alejandro was still at work. After that, Alejandro would be relieving his mother's palliative carer. As the mother had stage 4 cancer, pancreatic, Cliff knew Alejandro's time with her was precious and he did not want to interrupt that. Roy, on the other hand due to the events in Derry, just didn't really feel like being sociable, even with his closest friends.

Dana wouldn't take no for an answer and fussed over the three men for the whole evening. It turned out that she had been correct. Roy realised that moping wasn't going to do anyone any favours, and Cliff thought that Argentina could wait until the following day. There was news to be shared, and he couldn't think of a better place to do so.

Throughout the delicious meal, they had avoided any talk of the investigation. It was no surprise to any of them, as the quality of Dana's food, along with the convivial atmosphere, made them not want to discuss the two murders. The scallop starter had been served with a small glass of Sauvignon Blanc and the main course of Beef Wellington had demanded a full-bodied Shiraz. Dana knew their preference for cheese and biscuits for dessert, so had got Chas to open a new reserve port. Now coffee was served, and Dana had gone into the study for her regular family and friends girlie zoom call, the three men turned to the real subject at hand.

'How are you feeling?' Chas asked, realising it was a question he had been dying to pose all evening. He had held back because he hadn't told Dana everything. She was a perfect mother hen and a solid sounding board if the chips were down, but this was something on a completely different level. He certainly wasn't going to worry her unnecessarily.

'By all accounts, lucky to be alive,' sighed Roy. 'Doesn't seem real.' The others nodded, and Cliff grabbed him by the elbow. He wanted to show his support and this gesture did so without appearing too soft. 'Also feel devastated to think that Sinead is dead due to our investigation.'

'We can't know that for certain,' interjected Chas.

'Well, they can't think of any other reason,' answered Roy. 'They haven't had a bombing for decades.'

'Who was this guy then?' Cliff knew that wallowing in what happened to poor Sinead wouldn't move them on. And he was bloody determined, if not a little frightened, to solve this riddle. 'Chas, can you start us off?'

They spent the next hour sharing their information and bouncing ideas off each other. Cliff acted as a ringmaster, making notes and checking the information he had put down was correct. They each became totally absorbed and any anxiety they may have been feeling was replaced by a genuine interest in finding out more about the real Paddy Cullen.

As they sank back into their chairs, having a final large brandy, Cliff read back his notes, glad in the knowledge that an Über would be taking him and Roy home.

'So,' begun Cliff, 'thanks to Chas and Bertie, we know that Paddy was really James Paisley. Born in Ayr on 5th November 1951. Although he was born in Scotland, his heritage is Northern Irish Protestant. He joined the Royal Scots Regiment in 1970, and in 1975 trained for, and later became a soldier in, the SAS. Although his file is heavily redacted, again for this we owe Bertie big time, he served in Northern Ireland in the late 1970's and took part in the Falkland War, where he won the South Atlantic Medal.'

'Yes, we were lucky there,' interrupted Chas. 'Had his wife not known the former head of the SAS, Mike Wilkes, we couldn't have been so sure as to why there was so much information blacked out in that file.'

'Indeed,' continued Cliff, looking back at his notes. 'Thanks to Colonel Wilkes' information about SAS soldiers being used for clandestine work during the troubles, we can link that to Roy's investigation. He was identified from the picture in his army file appearing as Padraig O'Toole, a supposed paramilitary member of the Provisional IRA, lodging with Catholic sympathisers in Derry.'

'Yes, Mary and Brian somebody,' said Roy. 'With the bombing, I didn't get to follow that up.'

'Don't worry, my friend,' replied Cliff, in a soft tone. 'Thanks to you we have moved on a lot. Finally, we know that this O'Toole disappeared in 1980 almost as quickly and mysteriously as he turned up.'

'Perhaps his cover was blown,' mused Chas.

'Or his mission was completed,' added Roy.

'Let me just finish this summary off,' said Cliff, 'and then we can spend a bit more time on conjecture.'

'And work out what we need to do next,' enthused Chas, taking another sip of his brandy.

'Exactly. Now my investigation showed us where he went that could be of interest. Spain was probably only for bowls, just like lots of local destinations on his SatNav, but Argentina obviously may show some links to his army career and certainly piques my interest. As for Switzerland I think that might be the money trail.'

While he paused, Chas waded in. 'Yes, as someone who served in the army, why didn't he draw a pension? He was certainly eligible.'

'Well, it certainly was fortuitous finding the tattoo parlour in Weedon. The professional standard alphanumerical tattoo screams Swiss bank account, as do the large cash deposits into his bank account.'

'Don't forget the other tattoo,' said Roy. 'It implies he had two children, but we haven't found evidence of any long-term relationship.'

'Good point.' Cliff looked proudly at his friends. 'We need to dig deeper. Let's get together after golf tomorrow. I've heard from Joss that the course should be open in the morning.' Chas and Roy nodded in agreement. Joss, who was Percy John's nephew, worked in the pro shop at the club and he always kept Cliff and Mack, as regular playing partners of Percy, in the loop.

Thirty minutes later, Cliff and Roy were stepping, or in Roy's case slightly staggering, out of their Über. Cliff felt really protective of his lodger. Had things been different, then Roy might have not been staggering, or listing, next to him as he fumbled for the keys to the annex.

Chapter 10

Cliff had long since accepted the requirement to use online websites to help him find new 'friends'. Of course, the anonymity, which such sites afford its users, meant that Cliff had frequently been lied to, or even left waiting in cafés and hotel lobbies, with his 'date' having no intention of showing up. It had soon become clear that the profiles, blatantly fictional when it came to some, had to be read with a huge pinch of salt. There had also been an element of hit and miss when it came to the websites or applications themselves. Two of the more popular ones, Grindr and Fabguys were little more than a marketplace for anonymous hook ups and sex. A real meat market, more akin to the rough and tumble of early mornings at Smithfield's than anything you would find in your village high street.

Cliff had initially satisfied his needs with cruising, and the trips to Birmingham. And then he had found Doug, the love of his life. While going through the long grieving cycle for Doug, he had tentatively explored various online sites, and when he felt it appropriate to move on, he settled on Cuffmos and Silverfogies. These he felt best suited his needs, to find like minded older men who could offer much more than the physical. He doubted he would ever find another Doug, but cumulatively maybe three or four special friends with benefits might fill the void.

When he first went online to try to fill the massive hole left by Doug's death, Cliff hadn't really been thinking about anyone, or anything, else other than meeting his own needs. This selfishness wasn't really reflective of his true nature, but grief changes people. At least in the short term. One of the first people he started to correspond with was Keefe Waddlesworth, a 70-something fellow bowler from near Hitchin. Being an ex-headteacher, Cliff felt he might have found a kindred spirit. Even though Keefe was married, Cliff had assumed the marriage, like many for people of that age, was sexless and lacking the intimacy that Keefe was looking for. It was only during one of their Skype calls, fully clothed of course, when Keefe explained he would 'see to' his oversexed wife a few days prior to their first meet, thus ensuring he would be fit and able to perform with Cliff. Cliff was horrified to see how this man was prepared to manipulate his wife of over forty years. Not wanting to be part of such a relationship, particularly one where Cliff himself was being seen as a mere cherry to Keefe's sex life, Cliff let his would-be lover know exactly how he felt. From that moment onwards, Cliff resolved never to get involved with a partnered man, no matter how much he might proclaim the loneliness he feels within his relationship.

Cliff's two preferred dating sites brought him some short-term satisfaction and one long-term 'special friend', Javier in Spain. However, nothing remains in fashion forever, so as the popularity of these websites waned, a new one appeared in their stead. Oldgingerspice was currently the 'site du jour', and Alejandro was eventually identified as a potential replacement for poor unfortunate Javier, who had recently had to be admitted into an old people's home in Seville.

Cliff looked at his watch and sighed. Javier was now a shadow of his former self. His ebullience and machismo had once made their time together so special, but now in the aftermath of the pandemic, long-covid had taken its toll and Javier now looked 15 years older and 20 kilos lighter. It was Javier, out of love for Cliff, who had proclaimed the end of the physical side of their relationship. Cliff had resisted initially, in a state of virtual denial, but when Javier had sold his apartment overlooking the Mediterranean to pay for the care home, Cliff had had to admit defeat. He was, however, determined to make their friendship endure and, with the help of the the carers in the luxury facility, they still had a monthly video call. It was always a joy and never hard work for Cliff, but the quality of their conversations had diminished in recent times, as rampant dementia was cruelly taking control.

    In the short time he had known Alejandro, Cliff found him to be fastidious time wise, and with five minutes remaining before their scheduled call, Cliff let his mind wander back to the events of that morning. The clubhouse had been heaving, full of elderly men of all shapes and sizes, united in a collective relief to be able to play golf once more. The 9-hole winter series competition was popular with the Seniors Section as it afforded them regular organised golf throughout the winter, but in a shorter format making it more accessible to all, should buggies be banned. Cliff had considered himself fortunate to have been drawn with his weekend playing partners,

Mack Merlin and Percy Johns. As always there had been a small £2 side bet which made for some friendly rivalry. They all knew that this was the only prize available to them, because, due to the ridiculously high handicaps of many in the section, there were always 2 or 3 scores which even Tiger Woods would be unable to beat. It had been chilly out on the course, but not too cold due to an absence of wind, and the conditions were tricky with lots of muddy areas and some standing water on many of the holes. Despite this the three-ball hadn't stopped laughing for the whole nine holes. Back in the car park, Percy and Mack had handed a smug looking Cliff his winnings and then departed. This was no great surprise to Cliff as they rarely stayed to socialise after the round was over. Percy was always wary of upsetting his wife by being away any longer than necessary, besides which their miniature Schnauzer, Dozy, would be needing her daily lunchtime walk. Mack, on the other hand, would have stayed, but his elderly mum, now 101 years old, lived alone and he would be spending the next few days at her house, almost two hours away, making sure she had everything she needed until he returned the following week.

Chas and Roy were playing in separate groups about thirty minutes behind Cliff. That meant he could have a leisurely coffee before the three of them would find somewhere to plan their next moves in detail. Removing his hat as he entered the lounge area, he instantly recognised the bombastic tones of Bulldog. 'This country wouldn't be going to the dogs if we still had National Service. The kids these days don't know they are born. Take the bloody computer game controllers out of their hands, and put real rifles in them. Once they feel the recoil of an SA80 on their shoulder. That will make them stop and think. And as for all the knife crime and stabbings ......'

Cliff smiled, thanking his lucky stars that he rarely had to play with the pompous prick. The fact that his chosen audience for the day were members of the self-satisfied Committee made him smile even more. They were up for reelection in a few months and knew how influential Bulldog could be. They certainly didn't want to be on the wrong side of him until then. To all intents and purposes, Bulldog had them there as virtual prisoners. And he was loving every minute. As he bought a cappuccino from the machine, Cliff watched them, eyes glazed over, nodding in agreement. He could almost imagine them jabbing their thumbnails into other fleshy parts of their hands in an attempt to force themselves to focus, and not nod off.

In the far corner, Cliff spied the beckoning arms and friendly faces of Paul Frienden, Royston

McPartick and Tim Connolly – crap golfers to a man but great company. Together they spent a very enjoyable half an hour recounting stories of historical golfing misfortunes intermeshed with a few short-lived successes.

Finally, Cliff spotted Chas and Roy putting their clubs into their cars and turned to make his excuses. However, they weren't needed as the recent topic of the pros and cons of breakfast versus brunch had made them realise how hungry they were. And the local greasy spoon was calling them. Cliff, despite a slightly rumbling tummy, politely turned down their invitation and ordered a pot of coffee for three.

Having been mother, serving the coffee from the coffee pot, and patiently waiting for Chas and Roy to finish their tales of golfing woe, particularly long and particularly woeful in Chas' case, Cliff was finally able to get the conversation back to the investigation. It was decided that Cliff was to work on the Argentinian connection. It couldn't be a mere coincidence or ignored, that Paddy (they still used the name they had known him as, rather than Paisley) had served there in the Falklands war, and afterwards had been there on several occasions. Cliff didn't mention Alejandro by name but told the others he might have a useful acquaintance in Buenos Aries. Whenever Cliff mentioned his acquaintances, Roy and Chas knew what he really meant. All they wanted for their friend was happiness, so they never probed, nor did they judge.

Chas, along with Bertie if he were up for it, was going to follow up on the SAS angle, while Roy was going to go back to Derry, to find out more about the enigmatic Padraig O'Toole. They both decided to wait until after the weekend to get things going. Roy for example wouldn't be going too early in the week as he wanted to tie in his trip with Sinead's funeral. Chas and Cliff, fearing for his safety, begged Roy to stay in Daventry and use video calls, but Roy was adamant he needed to go in person. He had already spoken to Michael and his family, and as well as being happy to host him, they were confident they could guarantee his safety. Chas and Dana had plans with her family from Nottingham that weekend, and waiting a while would give Chas time to organise things with Bertie. Cliff was the only one hoping to make some progress before the weekend, hopefully that evening.

The screen of Cliff's laptop burst into life and was, at the same time, accompanied by the annoying Skype ringtone. Normally, Cliff preferred WhatsApp video calls on his phone, but knew his overseas friends tended to use Skype. Telling himself to remember to look at the settings after the call, to see if he could change the ringtone, Cliff accepted the call and Alejandro's face appeared large in the centre of the screen. They hadn't known each other long and Cliff still had to suppress a gasp every time he saw Alejandro's handsome visage. Despite being the same age, Alejo had immaculate ice white hair, which beautifully highlighted his wonderfully tanned Hispanic cheek bones and bright blue eyes. The frown, which had been briefly on his face, clearly waiting for Cliff to appear on his screen, quickly disappeared to reveal some brilliantly white teeth, which wouldn't be out of place on a toothpaste advert. Cliff, unconsciously glanced down at his smaller thumbnail image in the bottom right corner of the screen and wondered what this gorgeous man saw in the stocky Englishman who used a high-angled webcam to reduce the amount of chins. Instead of a brilliant head of white hair, Cliff's cropped salt and pepper hair was more reminiscent of a badger. Or maybe, even worse, a skunk.

Alejo had a wonderful command of the English language, albeit with the heavy accent of a Hispanic who had never left their homeland, so communication between him and the former Spanish teacher was never an issue. Anybody eavesdropping in on the next fifty minutes would have been both confused and amazed to see the seamless way each of the two would switch from one language to another, intuitively knowing which one helped most at the time. Having discussed the usual topics, Cliff started to tell Alejo of the investigation. They had never discussed the Falklands War before, and Cliff left that piece of the puzzle to the end. Alejo took the statement with the unflinching poker face of someone who worked quite high up in the Argentinian civil service, but when he saw where the conversation was going, he held up a hand to stop Cliff from going any further.

'So, you want me to abuse my position,' his accent made that word seemingly last forever, until he finally continued, 'and maybe put my job on the line to find out about your army's illegal incursions into my country, and furthermore to trace the activities of this dubious man when he later entered our country.' He stopped speaking and stared intently at Cliff, who clearly hadn't thought this through and was squirming red faced in his chair.

'Well, if you put it like that,' stuttered Cliff, 'then I can see I'm asking too much.' Cliff wasn't sure what else he could say.

Alejo pinched his lower lip in contemplation. 'If you come here next week and we have a wonderful weekend together, then I will do my best to find answers to your questions.

Cliff smiled. 'Sexual blackmail? I like it.'

Both of them spent the next twenty minutes, talking excitedly about what lay ahead. Cliff had been planning to try to go there later in the winter anyway. Looking at Alejo, who wouldn't? Having blown extravagant kisses to one another to finish the call, Cliff went onto Expedia and booked his tickets. Premium Economy. He knew he'd need to sleep during the flight, because he might not get much when there.

Chapter 11

Chas was relaxed after a surprisingly enjoyable weekend. When Dana had mentioned a few days away with her sister, he had feared the worst. Sandra was the polar opposite of Dana, opinionated and domineering, and the thought of staying at her house in Bingham had sounded like purgatory. Dana, knowing Chas so well, had taken great delight in playing up to his barely suppressed negativity, only revealing the truth as he was entering the destination on his SatNav. Instead of a claustrophobic couple of days in the semi-detached house, which she had lived in with her husband, Joe, since they married, they were going to a luxury hotel next to the Royal Horticultural Society garden in Bridgewater, near Manchester. Chas had always wanted to visit this new and innovative garden, so when Dana spotted the deal on Groupon she knew what she had to do. As it was Sandra's pearl wedding that month, she decided to treat her only sister as well. Chas and Dana had spent two full days exploring every nook and cranny and the only time their paths crossed with Sandra and Joe was in the hotel restaurant. Chas figured that sharing a table with the overbearing Sandra was small price to pay for what was otherwise a real treat for him. Besides, he did feel a bit sorry for Joe, who was alright when out of earshot of his wife.

The bowls match on the Monday had been great fun. Murray had rediscovered his form and, with their star player Mick Wartherton as skip, Chas had not felt the usual pressure he experienced when playing with Cliff and Roy. The team they massacred was called Llamedos. He knew it looked like a Spanish word, so he had asked Cliff for a translation. Cliff just smiled and replied. 'Read it backwards.' *Sod 'em all.*

Chas was still smiling at this naughty, but imaginative, wordplay as he pulled up in front of Bertie's house in Barby. Before setting off for Lancashire, the ever-organised Chas had phoned Bertie to update him on the investigation, and then to ask for his help once more. Bertie, who had greatly enjoyed the day at the Imperial War Museum, didn't have to be asked twice. He had nothing planned until a Caribbean cruise over Christmas and was more than happy to use his contacts to find out anything further about James Paisley's time in the SAS. When he and Dana had returned on the Sunday, there was a message on the landline from Bertie asking Chas to call as soon as possible. In that call Bertie explained that he had again been in contact with Lt. Colonel Mike Wilkes. Mike, apparently, had been cryptic in his response, but suggested that they might find out something interesting if they were to go to the Black Boy pub in Credenhill on Tuesday evening. Chas panicked when he heard that, as it was less than 48 hours away. Bertie laughed and informed him that he should calm down. Bertie had already booked them two single rooms in the pub. 'We will be staying in the annex, as the pub itself is fully booked. Some sort of celebration, it seems.'

Having stashed Bertie's kit bag in the boot. 'I normally take a small wheelie carry-on suitcase for short stays,' he shared as he handed the bag to Chas, 'but felt something from my army days could be an icebreaker.'

'Well, I suppose having your name and rank in plain view could save some explanations,' agreed Chas.

Having answered Bertie's follow up questions about what happened to Roy in Northern Ireland, Chas felt he needed to know more about their destination.

'I know it is in Herefordshire and the SAS train there, but why does Mike have us going to Credenhill?'

Bertie explained that Credenhill was the location of the Stirling Lines Garrison, the current home to the Special Air Service. He added. 'Of course, that's only since 1999. Before then it had been used as an RAF training school. Paisley will have trained at Bradbury Lines, a garrison which has since been decommissioned.'

'So you think this celebration at the pub is linked to the SAS?' Chas asked.

'Would have thought so,' answered Bertie. 'Can't see another reason why Mike would have sent us there.'

As they got closer to Credenhill, the landscape changed significantly. No longer were there major A roads, nor were there many urban areas to drive through. In fact, for mile upon mile, there was an obvious absence of dwellings of any kind. Chas remembered the programmes and documentaries he had seen about the SAS and its training regime based on survival and mental fortitude. 'It'd be bleak out here with nothing to eat and no warm bed to sleep in,' Chas thought, his body giving into an involuntary shudder.

Credenhill itself broke the illusion of starkness and isolation. The only fast-food establishments seemed to be fish and chips or Chinese takeaway based, with the centre lacking charm. Amid the backdrop of new housing estates, St. Mary's church stood out proudly against a rather uninteresting skyline.

The Black Boy, it turned out according to the sign, which was gently swaying in the wind, wasn't inappropriately named from the days of slavery or bigotry, but after a young chimney sweep. They pulled up in the car park behind the pub, close to the more modern annex. Chas, ever pragmatic, thought it logical that as they were to be staying there, then they wouldn't have to carry their bags as far. To his consternation, he noticed Bertie grab his kit bag from the boot, and then follow Chas to the rear entrance of the pub. As if he were reading Chas' mind, Bertie explained. 'I brought it here to advertise my credentials. If nobody sees it, then I might as well have left the bloody thing at home.'

There was nobody at the reception desk, so they followed the instructions on the sign, and rang the bell. While waiting, Chas picked up a brochure about the pub from a revolving rack next to the bench seat where he had settled himself. It was clear from the first look that the pub had history, but he hadn't realised quite how old it was. Built in the late 17th century, after the Pandy Inn in Doorstone, it was the second oldest pub in the county. Initially, it had been called the Fighting Cocks, but in the mid-eighteenth century it changed its name to the Black Boy, when a young chimney sweep had accidentally been burnt alive while cleaning one of the four chimneys, which were needed to provide warmth for the pub and its patrons. Chas found the reason more grisly than commemorative and shuddered as he imagined the plight of the poor lad, who probably, having been denied proper schooling, had been forced to work in the most narrow and uncomfortable of locations. To die in such a way beggared belief. Chas was glad he hadn't been alive in such awful times where class and entitlement ensured the ordinary man had no real chance to thrive or even just to improve their circumstances. 'Flipping heck,' he thought to himself, 'I'm becoming Roy.'

A young woman in her early twenties promptly arrived. She was dressed in what Chas decided was the uniform for the pub. In fact, it was similar to ones he had seen in many other hospitality venues. Her dark brown hair had been pulled back to form a ponytail, and she was dressed totally in black with a smart tailored jacket on top of a functional mid-length dress. Chas, thanks to the miracle of his cataract operations, could just about make out the writing on her badge. 'Elsa, Assistant Manager'.

'Can I help you?' Her voice carried the smile which had just appeared on her face.

'Yes,' replied Bertie, placing his kit bag on the desk, ostensibly to get out a hard copy of the booking from a zip pocket, 'we have two rooms reserved in the name of Colonel Bloomsbury. I think we are in the annex.'

Elsa tapped a few keys on the keyboard, which was on a level below that of the main desk and stared at the screen.

'We have you in rooms 115 and 116,' she said, looking at Bertie. 'Dinner and breakfast are included. Breakfast is served between 7.30 and 9.30 am and there are two sittings for dinner, the first at 7pm and the second at 8.30pm. Do you have a preference?'

Without consulting Chas, Bertie answered. 'The first sitting will do my dear. We aren't as young as we used to be. Early to bed, early to rise.'

'Are you here for the SAS celebration?' Elsa was looking at the kit bag as she ventured this question.

'No, didn't know anything about it,' lied Bertie. 'Same army, but different part. Still it's always nice to catch up with others who have served. Are there many here this evening?'

'I think about fifty are attending the dinner, and half of them are staying here tonight,' replied Elsa. 'There is only one long bar, so if they are having a drink before or after the meal, you could see them there.' With that, she handed Bertie the keys for the rooms.

'Hope you didn't mind me choosing the first sitting for dinner,' said Bertie, as they were walking across the car park. 'I felt it better to eat earlier, then we are free to mingle, so to speak.' He couldn't suppress a small laugh. Chas could tell Bertie was really enjoying himself, and in his element.

Their rooms were not adjoining, but directly opposite one another. 'Now I suggest we take the opportunity to have a quick doze, followed by a shower,' explained Bertie. 'Mike has afforded us a wonderful opportunity to meet so many former members of the regiment. We need to take advantage of it.'

Chas nodded and, having agreed to meet at 6.30pm, they entered their respective rooms. Chas fully intended to do what Bertie suggested, but first he needed to call Dana. Although they were often apart, Chas would always call her as much as he could. Roy would call him a 'soft bugger', but Chas didn't mind. They had something special, and he treasured it.

....

Chas smiled. The alarm clock provided on the bedside table had just ticked over to show 6.30pm, and at precisely that moment he heard three sharp raps on his door.

'Now that is military precision. Shame Roy doesn't possess such traits,' he mused.

He had just checked his appearance in the full-length mirror and knew that he would pass muster in Dana's eyes, but then that was love. He opened the door to see Bertie patiently waiting outside, and instantly felt underdressed. Despite wearing beige ironed chinos, an open-necked formal light-blue shirt and a fawn tailored single-breasted jacket, from Burberry's no less, he looked like a tramp in comparison. Bertie hadn't gone the full hog, army wise, but his accessories just oozed a pride from a life spent in one of the services. He wasn't wearing any medals on his dark double-breasted blazer, nor was he sporting a beret. Yet, his tie, presumably depicting his regiment, tightly positioned against his fastened top button, together with his immaculately polished black shoes, made one think immediately that this man had served.

'You're looking smart,' said Bertie, diffusing the situation he had quickly assessed from the somewhat panicked look on Chas' face. 'Much prefer that look. Smart but comfortable. Only dress like this for reunions or on Remembrance Day. Of course, I have to get the old gongs out too, then. Thought this look would break the ice without being too over the top.'

Chas was impressed with both his logic and the fact that he glossed over being awarded medals himself. There was a lot to like about this man. Chas had few close friends, but many acquaintances such as Bertie. He decided there and then to spend more time with him. If Bertie were amenable to that, of course.

They had been given a nice table next to one of the restaurant's very small leaded windows. The menu was both varied and tasty, thanks to a newly recruited head chef. The only criticism was that the service had been a little slow, but they suspected this might have been down to the celebratory meal going on in the long room upstairs. They had planned, chatted and planned some more as they munched their way through the three courses. Even though they had meant to be abstemious, so that their heads would remain clear for the task at hand, there was an empty bottle of Australian Shiraz on the table and a half-full glass of brandy in front of them as they were ordering their coffees.

Chas looked at his watch. 'They will have to have a quick Ryanair type turnaround to get this table ready for the second sitting.'

'I think the meal upstairs was due to start at 7pm so they should have received their mains by now. That means they can deploy more people down here for a while. I may have spent most of my time in a tank regiment but, as I approached retirement, I was an officer in the Commando Logistic Support Squadron,' he added seeing Chas looking a bit confused. 'I suppose those behind the line positions are often filled with experienced officers on the way out.'

'It sounds to me like you could still do a bloody good job,' replied Chas.

'Let's get down to the bar and find ourselves a good centrally located table.' Bertie reached into his blazer's inside pocket and took a £20 note from his wallet. 'They may have been a little slow, but the staff was very attentive. We can take our brandy down with us.'

Two more brandies and another coffee later, the bar started to fill with people from the celebration. To Chas' uneducated eyes, they looked like a real cross-section of ordinary men. As well as being different ages, their appearance was eclectic. Clearly the dress code was only smart casual, with nobody wearing any sign of a uniform, and as for their hair, crew cuts were clearly not a pre-requisite for former members of the SAS. Indeed, some of the guests looked like they had over-compensated for the former restrictions of their coiffure.

The plan had been to occupy one of the larger tables, not far from the bar, so that it would encourage people to sit on the same table as them, facilitating conversation. Unfortunately, thirty minutes later Chas and Bertie were still sitting on their own as all the other tables were filling up. Chas was beginning to feel despondent and started to fidget in his chair. His dip in optimism, though unspoken, had been perceived by Bertie, who stood up.

'Think we need a plan B,' he whispered to Chas. 'Afraid we will have to have another brandy. Back in a minute.' Chas watched Charlie circle around two newcomers to the bar. He could have gone straight across to the bar, but obviously had wanted to position himself directly in their eyeline. Sure enough, he quickly had managed to engage them in conversation, and to Chas' delight, they followed Bertie, with their drinks in hand, back to the table. Chas' new drinking companions turned out to be former SAS officers: Lieutenant Rick 'Tweeter' Finch and his former commanding officer, Captain Alex 'call me Ding-Dong' Bell. Despite that request, Chas refrained from using that rather embarrassing moniker as the initial conversation revolved around Bertie's service. It had been the tie, which had broken down any barriers at the bar. Tweeter's, now sadly departed brother, Chaff had also served in the tank regiment. Apparently, he, like Bertie, had been on tour in Aden in the 1960s. It had been there, during the tricky and dangerous Yemen campaign, that Chaff had been mortally wounded by a sniper, before finally succumbing to the wound a few days later in the mobile military hospital. Bertie apparently had still been training at Sandhurst and didn't get out to the Middle East until six months after Chaff's death. Bertie continued to allow the focus to be about himself and kept the others around him entertained with anecdotes from Cyprus and West Germany, where he had spent most of his time.

Chas was so enthralled that it was only when Ding Dong asked why they were there that he also came back to the present and remembered what they were trying to achieve. Having gained a degree of camaraderie from the two former officers, Bertie gave them the pre-planned story, how their former SAS friend James Paisley had died and that they were trying to locate any family he may have had. Sensing a degree of hesitation, Bertie quickly dropped the name Mike Wilkes into the conversation. This relaxed them at once, and Chas was overjoyed to hear that they both remembered Paisley.

'Odd cove, but brilliant soldier,' said Ding Dong.

'Yes, I remember he trained at Bradbury Lines,' added Tweeter. 'He started off in A squadron, but soon was cherry picked for Z squadron.'

'Z squadron?' Chas enquired, speaking almost for the first time in twenty minutes.

'Yes, if you think the work of the SAS is hush-hush, then Z squadron is something else,' said Tweeter.

'Officially, they don't exist,' chimed in Ding Dong, tapping his nose in a conspiratorial way.

'So, you don't know what he did once he joined Z squadron,' persisted Chas.

'No, the SAS works in squadrons, or cells if you like, and it's very much on a need-to-know basis,' replied Ding Dong.

Tweeter started to look around the men sitting in the bar. 'Most of these guys served after Paisley,' he mused, 'but I'll tell you what. I'm pretty sure I've seen two of his fellow Z squadron muckers here. Now where are they?' As he said this, he stood up to get a better angle.

Bertie and Chas couldn't believe their luck, and impatiently waited for him to identify Paisley's former comrades. Their excitement waned as Tweeter sat down shaking his head. 'Sorry, can't spot them. Maybe they've gone to bed already. I'm certain I saw them checking in earlier. I've got an idea, let's have breakfast together first thing and we will point you in their direction.'

'Good idea,' agreed Bertie, trying not to display his disappointment. 'No former soldier turns down a full English when it's already been paid for.'

Chas and Bertie stayed a further forty minutes talking, to Chas' delight, about gardening and growing vegetables. It seems the amount of time gardeners spend outside, along with the self-subsistence of the hobby, greatly appeals to retired soldiers, in particular those of the SAS - who hold their own fruit and vegetable show every September. 'It's a funny old world,' thought Chas, as they crossed the car park for the final time that day.

....

Chas hated to admit it, but he always slept better when he was away from Dana on his travels. It wasn't that her constant gentle snoring stopped him from getting enough sleep. Somehow, that didn't worry him. In fact, he found hearing her, during the night, a source of contentment. It was her annexation of the bed that was the problem. Most people may toss and turn during the night, but they rotate roughly on a central axis meaning that they stay on their side of the bed. Dana, however, to Chas' disappointment, is a roller. At times, she is more like a steamroller, or maybe a Panzer tank, seizing territory throughout the night to finally cause Chas to find himself lying right at the edge of the bed. It didn't need a visit to a psychologist for him to understand his regular nightmare, one where he is falling off a cliff edge. He had thought of suggesting a bed with two independent mattresses but knew this might upset his wife. He certainly didn't want her to contemplate separate beds, or even rooms. That would be the start of the slippery slope to no more physical contact between them. It might not happen as much as it used to, or even as much as he might like, but it was a key ingredient to their relationship, which they both had always enjoyed.

So, it was a refreshed Chas who found himself tapping on Bertie's door five minutes before the agreed time. To his surprise, Bertie opened the door dressed only in pyjama shorts. Obviously, as a former soldier, he seemed totally blasé about the situation and asked Chas to come in.

'Sorry, bit behind this morning,' he explained, peeling off the shorts and reaching for some boxers, which were neatly laid out with some other clothes on a chair. He had done this with his back to Chas, and obviously hadn't realised that he was standing at an angle in front of the full-length mirror. Chas, a little embarrassed, averted his eyes from Bertie's accidental full-length full-frontal.

'Mike called this morning for an update,' he continued, unaware of Chas' slight discomfort. 'I told him about breakfast, and he was pleased that yesterday evening had been useful.'

'That was nice of him to do that,' commented Chas.

'He also had another idea after we had left.' Bertie now had all his clothes on and was starting to tie his shoes. 'He looked up the staff list at Stirling Lines and realised the current CO, Jeff Dukes, used to be his adjutant. We have an appointment with him at 11.00 am.'

'That's brilliant,' said Chas. 'Hope what he can tell us isn't redacted like in the files.'

'I think he will tell us all he can,' replied Bertie, putting on a light waterproof jacket to protect him from the morning shower, which had just begun. 'Mike saved his life in Kuwait. That earns you a lot of favours.'

The breakfast was served buffet style but as the four of them were there as the serving started, everything was piping hot and looked freshly cooked. The conversation picked up naturally once more as they waited for Paisley's two former comrades to arrive. However, as the food was consumed and time passed, Chas and Bertie sensed a degree of frustration on the part of their two new friends. The large clock on the wall showed it was already 8.30 am.

'I'm surprised they aren't here already,' said Ding Dong, looking at those already consuming their breakfast. There were about twenty, almost as many as Elsa had said were staying overnight. 'Soldiers are morning people and creatures of habit, even after they've left the army.'

'You don't have to stay any longer for us,' said Bertie, realising they might be waiting in vain. 'Already you guys have given us so much of your time.'

'We will give it 20 more minutes.' Tweeter was looking at the clock. 'Breakfast will almost be finished by then, and we need to be at the gardens at Hergest Croft this morning.'

Chas pricked up his ears. 'I've heard of them. They are supposed to be …….'

He was interrupted by Ding Dong's impression of a stage whisper. 'There they are,' he said quietly, looking at two burly men in their late 60s walking into the breakfast room. Chas sneaked a quick look and was instantly convinced that, despite their age, they were men you wouldn't want to mess with. There was something about the intensity in their eyes and the extreme focus they seemed to have, even when doing something as mundane as getting food.

As they sat down at the other end of the room with their selection from the hot buffet, Tweeter pulled out his phone. 'Last night, I did some research online,' he confided. 'The balding one is Private Tony Etches and the one with the grey buzz cut is Mark Bull.'

'I remember them now,' added Ding Dong. 'Etches known as Sketches is from Billericay and Pit-dog Bull is from Hull. Two great soldiers but absolute bastards if you get on the wrong side of them.'

'Thanks for this,' said Chas. 'We can take it from here. Get off to Hergest Croft. Looking at them, I definitely wish I were going with you.' He was smiling a little sheepishly.

The two former SAS officers shook hands and took their leave. 'Don't forget you have our emails. You must come up and stay with me and Dana. I'd love to know what you think of our allotment.'

'Definitely,' replied Ding Dong, with a friendly smile. 'We will be in touch soon.'

Chas and Bertie bided their time, having a second cup of coffee. 'We don't want to interrupt their breakfast. A sure way to upset someone,' said Bertie knowledgeably. The signal to make their move was when Tony Etches, obviously a slightly slower eater than Bull who was dextrously twirling a spoon in his left hand having already finished his breakfast, put his knife and fork on the empty plate, before pushing it away from him. Bertie was up like a shot and made his way swiftly over to their table.

'Sorry for the intrusion,' he started, 'but Lieutenant Finch said you were the guys who could help.'

'How so?' Mark Bull was the one who replied, but their wariness was clear and united.

'Lieutenant Finch led us to believe that you served with James Paisley,' answered Bertie.

Bull looked at his friend before answering. 'What if we did? Most of what we did with him is covered by the Official Secrets Act. Anyway, the poor sod died almost 40 years ago, literally within months of handing in his papers. We were going to form a personal protection company with him, but he was killed in that accident just months before we had completed our own tours.'

Bertie was taken aback by this and sucked in his breath, trying to find the correct words. 'I'm afraid your information is incorrect. We knew James Paisley as Paddy Cullen and he was killed only a few weeks ago in Daventry.'

A look of confusion spread across both of their faces. 'No, that can't be true. We both received a letter from his family solicitor in Ayr telling us of the accident.' Etches looked directly at Bull as he spoke.

'And we both got something from his will. Not much, but it meant a lot to us,' confirmed Bull.

Chas who had been standing quietly behind while this exchange had been happening, then helped Bertie to outline what had happened, and what they had subsequently uncovered.

Bull and Etches were economical with the information they could, or more likely would, share. They didn't mention Z squadron by name but alluded to being with Paisley in a special section, which carried out the most secret of missions. They were separated for a time, probably - Chas and Bertie decided during a debrief later - when Paisley had been masquerading as a soldier in the IRA. They said the three of them had been together during the Falklands war but wouldn't go into any detail. They affirmed that 'Jimbo' was a great soldier, hard as nails and an incredibly loyal friend. They had no idea why he might have faked his death. 'Might have been delayed PTSD,' suggested Bull. 'He might have lost his bottle and didn't trust himself to go into the personal protection business.'

Etches nodded and added. 'Yes, that would have been a source of great shame. Of course, it would be viewed very differently now.'

As Chas and Bertie were walking towards their rooms to prepare to check out, Bertie stopped and turned to Chas. 'I think there is a lot they weren't telling us. And I don't mean the Official Secrets stuff.'

'Agreed. I could have sworn I saw some anger in both of their faces when we were telling our story. Something doesn't sit right.'

Stirling Lines Garrison was only a short ten-minute drive from the Black Boy and lay in a wide valley to the side of the minor B road, which had brought them there from Credenhill. On the other side of the road was a rather picturesque fast-flowing stream. Having shown their driving licences to prove their identity to the armed sentries at the gate, they turned left towards the two-storey building. The internal guard at the main entrance had been forewarned and waved them past saying that the way to the CO's office was through the third door on the right.

An NCO greeted them in the outer office and asked them to sit on some wooden chairs, which lined the wall opposite. As they sat waiting, Chas looked around the rather sparse room. The only interesting feature was a map of the garrison, clearly showing the tiny runway that was on the far side of the building. In fact, the CO probably had a window looking out over the strip.

The phone on the desk rang once, obviously a signal rather than a call. Without bothering to pick it up, the NCO advised them that they could now go into the CO's office. Jeff Dukes was a tall athletic looking man. Probably in his late thirties, both his appearance and accent reeked of middle class, and he oozed testosterone. So much so, Chas noted, that his hairline had prematurely receded. He had obviously been well trained in man-management and his disarming nature soon had Bertie and Chas relaxed and talking freely.

'Well, that went well,' said Chas as they exited past the sentry gate.

'Mike must have really greased that pole for us,' agreed Bertie. 'I found it hard to believe how open he was.'

'I think it shows how high a regard Mike must have for you,' replied Chas, glancing at Bertie.

'At least, we certainly have had it confirmed that Paisley was undercover in Northern Ireland. What was surprising,' continued Chas, 'is that Z squadron were so key in the Falklands war, even going on secret missions to Argentina. Well, Tierra del Fuego, anyway.'

Chas' car exited the valley, going up past a small car park used by tourists as a place to take panoramic photos. The guys were excited by what they had just learned and so engrossed in their conversation that they didn't notice a dark SUV pull out of the car park and start to follow them. All the way to Daventry.

Chapter 12

Cliff opened his eyes and a broad smile spread across his face. Even through the jet lag induced haze, he could admire beauty. In this case it was the lithe olive-skinned body of Alejandro, which was unashamedly stretched out, naked in the bed next to him. Not wanting to disturb the exquisite scene, he mimicked the action of a reiki masseur, slowly and almost sensually tracing the body with his right hand, ensuring no contact was made. He didn't want to waken his new lover, not yet anyway. He wanted to enjoy the moment. His hands stopped over Alejandro's white maned chest, allowing his hand to oscillate in rhythm with Alejo's gentle almost inaudible breathing. 'My Latino stallion', he thought remembering their love making. His hand moved further down and stopped once more millimetres over Alejo's now dormant manhood. 'Well Shetland pony anyway.'

Allowing a feeling of total contentment to wash over him, his mind began to relive the previous 36 hours. Having paid for meet and greet at Heathrow airport, Cliff had arrived in plenty of time to allow for a relaxed check-in. As he normally flew economy class on European flights, he had been pleasantly surprised at the perks Premium Economy afforded him. A total journey of sixteen hours, including a brief stopover at Sao Paolo airport, was certainly made more bearable by the additional space and adjustability of the larger seats. Metal cutlery with the meals was also a nice touch, but it was the Argentinian Malbec, only available at the front end, or upstairs, in the Boeing 777, which allowed him to sleep for long enough to arrive looking fairly fresh.

Alejandro had been standing at the arrival's barrier. Cliff had spotted him instantly. Although not a tall man, his flourish of white hair and upright posture made him somehow stand out in the crowd. Cliff, who had dressed for a long-haul flight in a polo shirt and dark-grey chino styled cargo pants, was pleased to see that Alejo wasn't wearing the suit and tie he normally donned for work. Cliff was confused when Alejo rather formally reached out to shake

Cliff's hand, while at the same time offering to carry the medium-sized case. It was only when he whispered, 'we can hug each other soon' in English that Cliff realised even though Argentina was more liberal than many other Central and South American countries, Alejo's important role meant he had to be careful in public places.

The drive from the airport took only 25 minutes because, as Cliff soon found out, the roads were wide with plenty of lanes and therefore unencumbered by traffic jams. Alejo instantly relaxed when they exited the airport and got out onto the main road towards Buenos Aries. 'It's so good to see you in person finally,' he said touching Cliff's inner thigh. 'You are so handsome.'

Cliff felt a quiver of excitement go through his whole body. 'Don't they have decent opticians in Argentina?' It was typical of Cliff to make a self-deprecating statement when somebody lavished praise on him.

'There is nothing wrong with my eyesight,' laughed Alejo, moving his hand further up Cliff's thigh, only stopping just below the groin area. 'Nor my taste. Now for all the things I have in mind for you today, I need you fully awake and alert. Although I make a decent coffee, it is nothing compared to the 'café solo' they make at the small pastelería next door to my apartment block.'

The next 20 minutes flew by with Alejo pointing out the sights and providing any appropriate historical background. As they neared their destination, the area started to look much more upmarket, reeking of money. 'This is the area of town I live in,' began Alejo. 'It is called La Recoleta. I consider myself very lucky to live here.' A minute later, he turned left down into a subterranean car park, presumably underneath his apartment block.

Alejo and Cliff took the lift to the ground floor, where Alejo suggested Cliff should wait while he took the luggage upstairs. 'Won't be two minutes,' he promised. It felt more like ten to the slightly jet-lagged Cliff, who was happy for a few minutes alone to gather both his thoughts and his energy.

In the pastelería, Cliff excused himself and made his way to the toilets at the back. He didn't need to pee, but the wave of tiredness he had experienced in the lobby made him glad that he had acted on Roy's advice and had fished out a blister of tablets from his wash bag while waiting at the conveyor belt in arrivals. 'I'm not judging you,' Roy had begun when handing Cliff the tablets, 'but you aren't getting any younger and your friend over there may go at it like a rabbit,' He had smiled when emphasising the word friend. 'These are super strength Cialis, and they last for two days. Might be best to take one every 36 hours.'

Both Alejo and Roy had been correct. The espresso and doughnut, combined with the Cialis had worked wonders. Two hours later, Cliff was standing on the balcony of Alejo's 5th floor apartment admiring the view and contemplating how much you could find out about another person when you are naked and between orgasms.

'Are you ready?' Alejo called out. They had showered together to complete their first intimate time together, but then Alejo had needed to make a work call while Cliff put on some fresh clothes. Cliff turned to see Alejo looking more handsome than ever. Dressed in a light-coloured linen suit to complement a white shirt, Alejo looked more like a model than a civil servant. 'I have it all planned,' he smiled, holding up a piece of paper. 'Even allowing for much more bedtime.'

True to his word, Alejo gave Cliff an evening never to be forgotten. A taxi arrived and, while there was still daylight and under Alejo's direction, Cliff was shown the sights of Buenos Aries: from the Plaza de Mayo, the square which commemorates the revolution, that brought about Argentinian independence, to Palermo park, a smaller version of

New York's Central Park. In between, Cliff lost count of the number of galleries, museums and statues he saw on the way. Alejo even showed him the Congreso Nacional, not because the domed capitol was the seat of the national legislature, but because the building around the corner was where Alejandro himself worked. Cliff heard the pride in Alejo's voice when he pointed it out. He wanted to share in the moment by touching his new lover, but resisted, remembering they were back in the public eye. He would show his appreciation later.

They got out of the taxi in La Boca, an area known for its interesting and colourful architecture, which seemed even more upmarket than la Recoleta. The people, as well as the building, seemed to drip money, whether it be the immaculately coiffured hair, haute-couture clothes or expensive accessories such as Tag Heuer watches. Alejo showed his romantic side, as he must have remembered a previous conversation, where Cliff said he had enjoyed the best steaks ever when dining in Argentinian steakhouses in Spain. Suddenly, interrupting his narration about the six lane boulevards of the area, he stopped, turned and opened a door on his right. He ushered Cliff through ahead of him. The name 'Gaucho' was the only uninspired thing about this steakhouse. There weren't pictures or wallpaper on the walls of the entrance to the restaurant, but windows full of hanging meat. Each part of the butchered animals had a name card stating its breed, place of origin, and more importantly, the amount of time it had been ageing. Taste wasn't the only sense this restaurant heightened. There was live tango music playing in the background, and the presentation of the spectacular food was a feast for the eye. When the Bife de chorizo, a sirloin strip, the best cut according to the waiter, arrived, Alejo stood up and spoke. 'Do you trust me?' His smile and twinkling eyes told Cliff to say yes, so he nodded. Alejo went behind Cliff and tied a silk scarf across his eyes. As he did so, the band moved closer thus increasing the sound of the Tango. He heard Alejo say. 'Abre la boca,' which he did instantly. He felt something enter his now opened mouth and then a light touch on the underside of his chin instructing him to close his mouth once more. For an instant he recognised the texture of a small piece of meat inside his mouth, but that feeling gave way to an emotion, one of heavenly rapture. At the same time as the saliva in his mouth activated his taste receptor cells, the music cleverly reached a crescendo meaning that his senses were being attacked on multiple fronts. Attacked maybe, but in an amazing way. Cliff suddenly felt he was experiencing the essence of Argentina.

He would have been happy to have gone home after the restaurant, but Alejo was now incredibly relaxed and seemingly content. So much so that, as they turned left out of Gaucho, he forgot his rule about public intimacy and patted Cliff affectionately on the tummy saying. 'We need a little exercise to help the digestion.'

It was dark now and Cliff had no idea where he was, so he followed Alejo's lead. He soon found himself descending some barely lit stairs. As his eyes became accustomed to the dark, he noticed a few rainbow flags and then in the distance he heard more tango rhythms. Alejo stopped at the door and kissed him. 'You told me your guilty secret was Strictly Come Dancing. And your favourite dance was?' With that he paused.

'The Argentine Tango,' finished Cliff, who simultaneously thought. 'What have I let myself in for?'

Apparently, 'Chulo' is a gay night club at the weekend, but during the week it has theme nights, and as luck would have it, or maybe not in Cliff's mind, that night was Argentine Tango for beginners. He needn't have worried, because it turned out to be great fun.

Back now in the present, Cliff lay staring at Alejo's manhood. He remembered the two of them mastering basic 'ganchos', fumbling at more technical 'ochos' and worrying they would end up black and blue. Just like in bed they had switched roles easily on the dance floor, ensuring the pleasure was shared.

Remembering this, Cliff started to blow gently over Alejo's slumbering Shetland pony. Sure enough, both it and Alejo started to stir. 'What a wonderful way to wake up,' he said, caressing Cliff's inner thigh. 'Remember if you want me to find out about this man, Paisley, I will need to access the server at work for a few hours.'

'We have time my sweet man,' replied Cliff, focussed on a different task.

Chapter 13

Roy wasn't the most patient of men. In fact, he was quite prone to irritability. Standing at an airport conveyor belt, waiting for the 'bloody lazy baggage handlers', was one of his many triggers. He had been standing next to conveyor belt number three for almost twenty minutes, and he could palpably feel his blood pressure rising. In the past he'd have just exploded, taking it out on whoever, or whatever, was next to him, regardless of their culpability. However, with the help of Cliff, he had recently tried to learn to diffuse such situations as soon as he recognised their appearance. 'You need to nip these negative outbursts in the bud,' Cliff had told him. 'Take yourself out of the situation to a happier place.' So there in amongst about 50 other frustrated travellers, Roy took himself back to the evening before, and into the arms of the gorgeous Judith.

He felt Judith had been playing hard to get, but that just made him more determined. 'Keep your eyes on the prize,' he kept reminding himself, as he ordered each cup of coffee at the bowls club. Whenever he thought of the prize, he couldn't help but eye Judith wistfully up and down like a keen house buyer, focussing on the two up and hoping eventually to get access to the one down. Of course, this not too subtle leering took place whenever she turned around to add the foaming milk to his latte. As she returned with the drink, she would always ask. 'Anything else, my duck?'

'How about a date?' Roy sometimes varied the sentence, but each had exactly the same meaning.

Judith had always declined his offer of a date, but seeing a sadness in his eyes that Wednesday morning, she had changed her question. 'What's wrong Roy?'

'You know I'm mad about you and would love us to go out,' he replied. 'Just for you to see the real me. I'm not the Lothario I'm painted to be.'

'I'm sure you're not. But why are you looking so sad today?'

'I'm going back to Ireland for almost a week, and it makes me sad that we still won't have had that date.' He had surprised himself with his honesty, but when it came to women he wasn't always in full control of his emotions.

Judith turned and looked at the calendar on the wall. 'Well, the club is shut this evening. For the carpet to be stretched and cleaned,' she said. 'I suppose if you offer me something so tempting I can't refuse…..' She tailed off the sentence, allowing Roy to finish it for her.

'I hear that new Turkish restaurant on the High Street is supposed to be good,' he ventured, grateful to have already pre-planned their first date. 'I think it's named after their pet. Ali Cat.'

Judith laughed. 'It's Alacati, Roy. The town where the owner was born. I heard his wife telling my hairdresser their story. It's a date then. I don't live far from there. You can pick me up at 7.30pm.'

Roy looked like he had won the lottery. His beaming smile didn't alter when she added. 'It's a first date. Don't expect too much.'

The other 50 or so travellers, had they cared, would have witnessed a stark transformation in Roy. As he relived the previous day's events, the tension in his body subsided and the muscles in his face had relaxed, allowing a look of contentment to form on his face.

Roy had already seen Cliff off to the airport. His mind then turned back to his date with Judith. He had made an effort and was both well dressed, under the heavy winter's coat anyway, and on time. In fact, he had waited, stamping his feet to battle the cold, for five minutes to ensure that he arrived one minute early. Not too keen, but keen enough.

The food in the restaurant was plentiful and delicious and the conversation rotated about his life, past and present. His favourite subject. Even though he held out no hopes for too much intimacy after the meal, he ensured that he chose similar dishes to Judith. It conveyed a commonality between them. Something that he had learned in his four marriages, and all of his other dalliances, was that women liked men to have an overlap of tastes or interests. However false it may be. It also ensured that both of them consumed the same amount of garlic. Just in case he were to get lucky, he had raided his bedroom drawer and chosen the same dose of Cialis tablet he had gifted Cliff. If it were a sure thing then he would have gone for the max-strength Sildenafil, or Viagra. Much better in his experience for a one off go, so to speak, even if it did sometimes leave a headache. However, given the uncertain nature of the date, he knew the Cialis would ensure success and it took only half the time to work.

Fortunately, it still wasn't raining when he escorted her home. He was pleasantly surprised when she asked him in for a coffee. It was from an expensive Nespresso machine, just like the one George Clooney advertises. 'Maybe I shouldn't have shaved,' he had mused, while waiting for Judith to make the drinks.

He was even more pleasantly surprised when Judith sat next to him on the sofa. Even though it was a spacious two-seater, she sat close so that their legs touched. This part of a relationship was, in Roy's eyes, always the most stimulating. It made him feel like a teenager again, stepping into an amazingly exciting sexual adventure. It always made him think of the Meatloaf song, 'Paradise by the dashboard light'.

It was actually Judith who moved her head, and lips, towards Roy, stopping inches away. Roy didn't need a second invitation and his lips met hers. Being a true gentleman, Roy waited a full two seconds before gently easing her lips apart with his tongue. She didn't seem to mind and reciprocated. What happened after that was 'top half action' only. Roy had never really understood the American system of assigning bases, but he was ecstatic with how the evening had gone. Judging by their final kiss as he was leaving, he was guaranteed a home run next time.

The Cialis in his pocket then would be replaced by a Sildenafil. He almost wished it were raining as he went home, because he felt as light-footed as Gene Kelly.

Roy was now back in the present and, looking around, realised he was now on his own next to the conveyor belt. There was one case left on it, his. He picked up his suit-bag he had brought over as cabin luggage for Sinead's funeral and waited for his case to turn the corner. With all of his belongings in hand, he set off for arrivals and to find Michael Kelly and his son Seamus, who would be waiting for him.

....

Roy, who was once again sitting in the back seat of Seamus' car next to Michael Kelly, looked out the window to see the outskirts of Derry fast appearing. He couldn't believe they'd got there already. It only seemed a few minutes ago that Seamus had taken his case from him at the airport, having at first welcomed him with a friendly handshake. Then he had heard the now familiar voice of his new friend, Michael. He had reached out his hand for Michael to take, but instead the Derry-man had swamped him with a bear hug saying.

'Great to see you again, Roy. Let's get you back home. Siobhan has made something special, and she will have my guts for garters if we arrive late.'

Although the outward atmosphere towards seeing him was one of bonhomie, Roy was conscious to the fact that Seamus seemed to be in a state of high alert, constantly changing the direction of his gaze. Instead of being frightened or ill at ease about this, Roy was grateful to have the Kellys looking out for him. As publicans they were obviously successful. You don't keep a pub thriving for so long, particularly in the current post-pandemic economic environment, without being streetwise and intelligent. But as bodyguards they seemed pretty skilled as well.

Siobhan had pushed the boat out for Roy's arrival. A three course meal of smoked salmon, followed by roast Irish beef with all the trimmings started off the banquet. Both of these courses, neither of which were new to Roy, were exquisite in taste and presentation. Siobhan, who had made sure that she was sitting next to him, took great delight in telling Roy that the Salmon came from Lough Erne, farmed by her cousin Eugene. The cow, now working its way through their digestive systems, had been happily reared on a farm a mere two miles outside of town. A farm owned by her uncle Finn. Obviously, provenance and quality of product were key in these two courses, but it was the simplicity and tradition of the pudding, which was the highlight for sweet-toothed Roy. 'Fifteens', a basic looking traybake, is made with digestive biscuits, glacé cherries, marshmallows, condensed milk and desiccated coconut. Siobhan was more than happy to write out the simple, but delicious, recipe for the effusive Roy. Of course, being Roy, he had ulterior motives. He had been thinking, well maybe fantasising, about Judith and thought he might make it for her. It might even end up on the menu at her café in the bowls club.

'Right then,' began Michael, 'we need to go downstairs. There is someone down there you should meet.'

Roy looked at the Irishman, surprise on his face. This was the first he had heard of it. 'You didn't think all we had been doing was sitting here drinking Guinness and following the horses?' Michael continued, with a smile spreading across his face. 'You have a problem to solve, a friend to bury and we were determined to help you. This is only the beginning.'

Michael led the way downstairs, holding the door open for Roy to enter the bar area with him. He stood to Michael's right as the elderly Irishman surveyed the room and sought out his target.

'Over there,' he said, pointing at two men sitting at a table in the corner. 'There they are.' Before being able to ask who they were, he found himself trailing after Michael once more. As he approached the table, Roy recognised the man facing him as Michael's race-form studying friend. Michael sat down opposite his pal, and beckoned for Roy to take the vacant chair next to the other guy.

For a second, Roy did a double take thinking he had sat opposite a mirror, because the second guy looked almost identical to the other man, maybe, on reflection slightly less wrinkled and with a more obvious receding hairline.

Michael broke the silence. 'Now this excuse of a man,' he started, at the same time ducking a right-hander from the aforementioned 'excuse' is my oldest and best friend Joseph.'

'You won't be digging yourself out of that hole, you ol' sod,' laughed Joseph, taking a swig of his Guinness. 'Excuse of a man, be buggered.'

'Now,' continued Michael undeterred, 'his family, the O'Connells go back in Derry for generations.'

'That's right,' confirmed Joseph. 'We are the nearest thing to Derry royalty.'

Michael roared with laughter. 'Go away you daft eejit. Do you see what I have to put up with?'

Michael addressed this to Roy, who sat there still not sure what was going on. 'Local gossips and nosey Parker's, more like.'

Joseph shrugged his shoulder and took an even longer swig of his beer.

'Anyway,' continued Michael, 'after you went back to England, me and Joseph started trying to recall what we could remember about Padraig O'Toole and the family he stayed with.'

'Well, we had their Christian names,' added Joseph

'And where they lived, but although we were anti the Protestant oppression, we weren't really active in the fight,' said Michael tag teaming with his friend.

'It was need to know, you see,' Joseph was back leading the chat. 'The less the ordinary people knew, the less they could harm the cause.' Roy was now totally confused.

'Then Joseph had one of his rare moments of inspiration. He remembered that his little brother, Oisin, played Hurling with someone called Brian.' At this point they both stopped and looked at the fourth guy, who until then had just sat there sipping a small whiskey. Realising he was the grand finale of this production, Oisin cleared his throat.

'That's right, Brian and Mary O'Donovan had moved into the street a few years before in the mid-70s. He was a deadly man with the hurl, and after he joined our team we won the Ulster championship, three years running.'

Roy held up his hand. He needed clarification. 'Deadly? You mean he killed people with those funny little hockey sticks.'

Michael shrugged off the comment as cultural ignorance and replied for Oisin. 'No, Roy. Deadly is a slang term. It just means he was good at it.'

'Like Deadly Derek Underwood, at cricket,' said Roy, looking smug at being able to draw such a quick example. If he had expected any approbation, then he was sorely mistaken. Now it was the turn of the three men of Derry to look confused. Michael realising this tangential move was wasting time said. 'Go on, Oisin.'

'Well, off the pitch he generally kept himself to himself, but when we had an away game I used to pick him up. Sometimes he wasn't ready and his wife, Barbara, would chat to me. Always something trivial. It was like she was bored.'

'Maybe she was a neglected wife giving you the eye?' Joseph suggested.

'G'way outta that. She hardly even looked at me,' replied Oisin a little incensed.

'So, you used to take him in your car to the away matches?' Roy asked, now more in step with both the topic and the thick accent of the three men, who seemingly had forgotten to tone it down for their target audience.

'Yes. We talked mainly about the games. In anticipation on the way, and dissecting it on the way back. But, after one game in Belfast he looked shaken, less composed like.'

'Why was that?' Roy pushed.

'It was as we were leaving the ground. An RUC fucker called after us. I couldn't quite catch what was said, but it sounded like, "O'Donovan is that you?". Whatever it was, Brian speeded up and I followed. Most of the crowd was walking in the other direction towards the city centre, so we easily lost the copper and high-tailed it out of there. I decided not to say anything, not until we were out of the city. It would have been weird to say nothing, so I eventually asked what that had all been about. He said one thing, and it's stuck with me over the years. 'There is no worse bastard than a Catholic cop. He was an arse at school and even more of a cunt now'. He was so angry that he spat that out. He went on to say something else. I couldn't be certain, but I think he said 'It's a fucking shame he was off duty that night'.'

'What do you think he meant by that?' Roy enquired, not quite following.

'That he was from Belfast, and probably had been one of the Provos who had blown up the Queen Street Police Station.'

'So, you think that's why he moved to Derry, to avoid the search for the bombers,' asked Roy.

'Makes sense,' said Michael. 'Belfast became a virtual no-go zone, particularly in the Catholic areas, like Falls Road, for almost six months. They upped their stop and search, and more soldiers were flown over from West Germany to beef up manpower and security. I think even the staunchest sympathiser was shocked. 30 dead, including nine passing civilians. Collateral damage they called it, but it made a lot of people think for the first time.'

'So, we know their name and that the O'Donovans were almost certainly IRA but what about Padraig O'Toole?' In Roy's calculation, all they had confirmed was that the family they thought Padraig had been staying with were linked to the IRA.

'Well,' replied Oisin, 'this bit is where it gets a little funny, if funny is the correct word. Just before Christmas the hurling team was looking to go out together, for a seasonal celebration, like. The Captain of the team, Conor McGuinness, thought it'd be a hoot to pay homage to our top scorer, Brian, to go to see the newly released film, The Life of Brian. Everyone thought it was a great idea and wives, girlfriends or even friends could come along. Brian said that because his wife was heavily pregnant that he'd bring his lodger, Padraig.' Roy pricked up his ears and waited for Oisin to continue. 'Anyway, I was seated next to him in the bar and asked whether he played hurling. He said he had tried at school but his hand-eye co-ordination was crap. Bowls was his game.'

'Bowls!' Roy exclaimed. 'That's the proof Padraig was James Paisley. What happened to him? Do you know?'

'He disappeared. The army made a dawn raid on the house the following March. There was some resistance.' Oisin emphasised the word resistance. His voice clearly full of irony.

'Either that, or one of the fecking boy soldiers got scared and panicked,' interjected Joseph. 'Kids they sent us. Wet behind the ears, for feck's sake.'

'Anyway,' continued Oisin, 'neither Brian nor Mary left that house alive. Padraig wasn't there, and nobody in the area saw him again.'

'What about the baby? It'd have been born by then,' asked Roy, his voice full of concern.

'Babies,' corrected Oisin. 'There were twins, a boy and a girl. Just like Padraig they were never seen again.'

Everyone around the table went silent, taking in this shocking revelation. What happened to James Paisley, between the disappearance of his alter ego, Padraig O'Toole, and his arrival in Daventry as Paddy Cullen was still unclear. But that mystery was slowly being revealed. The bombshell that the newborn O'Donovan twins had disappeared as well. That had made everyone think.

'Would their disappearance ever be resolved?' Roy mused. He hoped so. The poor things.

Roy showed his gratitude by buying the next two rounds with the conversation turning to more mundane topics: sport; Roy's love life; their respective health problems; how many times they have to pee at night and finally back to Roy's love life.

'This Judith sounds a lovely girl,' said Joseph, standing up. 'She is well worth pursuing. Come on Oisin. We need to head off.'

'Yes, you need an early night too, Roy.' Michael was gathering the empty glasses to take them to the bar. 'You have a breakfast appointment first thing in the morning.'

'Really,' said Roy, also getting to his feet. 'Who with?'

'You'll see,' replied Michael, the smile on his face said he wasn't going to add any more.

Five minutes later, two other clients were paying their tab at the bar. Seamus took a credit card from the slightly older more heavier set man. They had been seated for over 90 minutes in the corner, and in that time had only drunk four non-alcoholic drinks between them. That was the only reason they had stood out, because Kellys was a drinker's pub. Not really for families or children. Even the wives and the girlfriends of the regulars would only go there under sufferance. For that reason, Seamus made sure he had been the one to take their payment. That way he could satisfy his curiosity. As they left the bar, through the side entrance, Seamus reflected on the two things his short conversation had revealed: they were from Belfast and they hadn't been honest. They said they were looking to expand their company and Derry seemed a great second market for their sportswear outlets. This wasn't what had troubled Seamus. It was the fact that the guy said it was their first time in the city. Seamus knew this not to be true. The large frame of the guy stood out in a crowd, with his cropped hair, bushy beard and scar above his right eye. Seamus had seen him around before, but for the life of him, he couldn't quite place where.

....

Michael tapped on Roy's bedroom door. 'Are you up and about, Roy?' He spoke through the door, not waiting for an answer. 'We need to leave in fifteen minutes.'

Roy replied, saying he would be down presently. In fact, he could have left the room there and then, but just wanted to gather his thoughts. He had debated whether to contact Cliff and Chas, deciding that Cliff would be either jet lagged, sleeping or doing something else in bed. He had been intrigued by Michael's tease last night. He thought it best to relay the information when he had all the facts rather than drip feed it as it came in. Having completed the triple S mantra his old university football coach had used when they went on European tours, 'shit, shave and shower. In that order', he had only needed to get dressed for the bitterly cold Derry winter's morning. Taking one final breath check, he sniffed the palm of his hand and went in search of Michael.

'Seamus has decided to join us,' pronounced Michael, as they walked to the car.

'That's great. I'm buying. You guys have been terrific and I can't thank you enough,' replied Roy. 'Wherever we are going, you should have anything you want.'

'There's no decision to make,' laughed Seamus. 'We will be having the Ulster fry, even you Roy. It's the best in Derry.'

Seamus pulled the car up across the road from the café. As he was putting money in the meter, Roy looked around and realised they were only fifty yards from the police station. The one he had been taken to after the explosion. He shuddered as he recalled that traumatic day.

'Come on,' urged Michael, 'there is a gap in the traffic.'

Grateful for the warmth that little bit of exercise had given him, he followed Michael into the café. He could hear the car door shutting and then the sound of Seamus' footsteps behind him.

The café was on the small side, with only about ten tables. Roy instantly recognised Declan O'Shaughnessy, the kind and helpful police sergeant, who had made that day a few weeks earlier so much easier for Roy than it could have been.

'Hi Roy, good to see you again.' Declan gestured for Roy to sit opposite him. 'I've taken the liberty of ordering Ulster Fries all around. You tell me what your investigation has uncovered so far and then I will add what I can.' By this time, Michael and Seamus had occupied the other seats.

'Wow! That is some breakfast,' exclaimed Roy as his plate was set before him. 'Talk about carb city.' He looked at the carbohydrate rich meal, including potato pancakes and soda bread. 'No wonder you chuckled when I asked for extra toast,' he continued, pointing the handle of his fork at Michael.

'Well, we thought you were hungry,' laughed Michael.

Roy used the pauses between mouthfuls to fill Declan in with what had been discovered in England, concluding with an account of the conversation the previous night with Joseph and Oisin.

Declan, who hadn't said a word throughout breakfast, pushed his almost empty plate to the side and started to speak. 'I remember hearing of the story of the missing twins now. I think I saw a documentary about it when I was in my teens. Apparently, there was a big outcry, with the press hounding the police, Army and Government even, to find them, and to explain their disappearance. Of course, they were never found. I suppose it could be resurrected as a cold case now,' Declan paused to gather his thoughts. 'Just like always, any exceptional and newsworthy event is superseded by another more dramatic or tragic one. So, given the bloody and volatile nature of the Troubles at that time, interest in the twins just waned or was transferred to something more current.'

'Do you have anything to add to what I've just said?' Roy knew Declan wasn't there just to comment on what was already known.

'Well, you are lucky I was seconded to the Met for a while, and built up some contacts in MI5. With their help, and some records online, I've put together a picture, rather sketchy maybe, of our man.'

'I never knew you went to the Met, Declan,' said Seamus, sounding rather amazed. 'For feck's sake, why did you bother to come back to this shit hole?'

'Why do you think?' Declan laughed. 'Better Guinness, and to keep the missus happy. She didn't want our kids to be schooled in an inner city monster comprehensive.'

'Fair enough,' replied Seamus.

'When you two have finished,' interrupted Michael.

'Right, I can confirm the O'Donovan's were on the run from Belfast. Apparently, he was right down the food chain, in the IRA, so was monitored rather than lifted. He was clearly trying to become someone more important in Derry. So, when Paisley turned up, posing as O'Toole, a soldier on the run himself, O'Donovan volunteered to take him in as a lodger. Keeping an eye on him at the same time, at least until he'd passed scrutiny.' The other three were all leaning forward, hanging on every word. 'He must have done some little jobs well enough to be trusted within the cell. So much so that he became part of an assassination attempt on the then Minister for Northern Ireland, Michael Alison.'

'I remember him,' interjected Michael. 'A right pompous Tory twat. Shame he wasn't killed.'

'Da!' Seamus was horrified. 'You didn't bring me up to think like that.'

'No, you are right son, but I hated the bastard. Sorry Roy.'

'I would blow up all Tories,' laughed Roy. Then he became more serious. 'So, Paisley's intel saved a minister's life? Wow!'

'Yes, it was a co-ordinated raid at five different residences. All confirmed by Paisley. He slipped out at 4.30am, and the raid happened fifteen minutes later. Unfortunately, the Provos traditionally kept weapons in their bedrooms, and in four of the five houses it became a shoot out, with the O'Donovans dying in one of them.'

'Any follow up on Paisley?' Roy asked.

'Nothing in the records, but we can assume that he went back to England and rejoined his regiment.'

Roy was true to his word and, after thanking Declan, he paid for the meal. He then followed

Michael and Seamus to the car. Declan remained behind to check his work emails.

'What now?' Roy asked, as he was getting into the car.

'Well,' replied Michael, 'we have one more meeting tomorrow. This afternoon has a great racing card. Do you like a bet?

'What do you think? I was the Mirror's stand-in racing correspondent for six months.'

Seamus interrupted them as they started to talk betting coups. 'One minute da,' he said, 'I've left my phone in there.'

'No worries,' replied Michael. 'Thank Declan again for us.'

Declan was surprised to see Seamus re-enter the café and sit down next to him.

'What is it?' Declan asked.

'Out there,' Seamus was almost shaking, 'I just saw a guy from the pub last night. He lied saying it was his first time in Derry. I knew I'd seen him before. I knew it, but couldn't remember where.' He paused, before continuing. 'Now I do.'

'Where then?' Declan sensed he was going to be told something important.

'Standing near the car park just after the bomb went off. I think he and his pal are after Roy. Come on, we might spot him if we are quick.'

Chapter 14

Cliff walked out, wearing only a clean polo shirt and light-coloured chinos, into a beautiful Argentinian summer's morning. The sky was blue with only a few wispy clouds off to the west. He smiled thinking of Roy and Chas, back in the UK, having to endure the arrival of the first 'Beast from the East', a recent hyperbolic moniker which the media used to scare the public. Both the press and TV always take great delight in inventing dramatic names whenever the cold weather from the continent is blown westwards over the North Sea. Having looked at the weather forecast online, Cliff surmised that this particular beast was not so much a violent man-eater ravaging all before it, but more akin to the reaction of a domestic pet, which had had its paw stepped on.

The rather sensual bout of love making that morning had given way to an overwhelming need to sleep, probably jet lag finally taking its toll. He had woken to find a note from Alejo on the pillow saying that he had left for work, where he was going to look into the mystery that was James Paisley. There were also suggestions for a late breakfast, either from supplies to be found in the kitchen or at local cafes. Cliff opted for some cereal and a coffee on the balcony. He knew Alejo wouldn't return until early afternoon so, having showered and dressed, he decided to explore the local area.

La Recoleta was both visually and culturally interesting. Cliff expected that there would be more than a smattering of shops, eating establishments, bars and galleries. In fact, all the places you would expect to find in an exclusive quarter of any cosmopolitan city, wherever it may be in the world. What Cliff soon appreciated was that there was a richness and variety in architectural styles, as he found when viewing the tombs of the massive cemetery, which had only recently reopened after the pandemic to the general public. Numerous white churches and the impressive Vatican embassy punctuated the skyline, with the large park providing an ecological balance.

Cliff found himself sitting on a bench in the park when he heard the familiar whistle of an arriving WhatsApp message. It was from Alejandro. He was heading home, and he had much to share.

....

Alejandro had made them both a strong black coffee and they were now sitting on the same side of the large oak dining room table. Alejo's laptop was open, receiving a charge from the wall socket, and in front of Alejo was a notebook. Cliff was trying to contain his curiosity, but he was sorely tempted to lean over and simply read his lover's hand-written notes. Fortunately, Alejo sensed his agitation, and, with a smile, began his report.

'I spent the first 45 minutes in my office accessing the immigration software to try to track his movements in Argentina.' Cliff nodded to show that he was being attentive, and at the same time appreciative of what Alejo had done for him. 'I can tell you that James Paisley never entered this country, not officially anyway.' He saw a look of disappointment on Cliff's face, so he kept going knowing that his next piece of information would be of significant interest. 'However, since 1985, Paddy Cullen has legally passed through our border control thirteen times. In fact, he seems to come here almost every two years. And never during our winter.'

'Flipping heck. I thought he came here, but so often! Any idea what he does, or where he goes when here in Argentina?' Cliff asked, his voice almost stuttering while trying to take this fact in.

'He always flies into Buenos Aries. That is the norm for virtually every foreign visitor, I think. During his first two visits we have records of him flying on to Ushuaia.'

'Ushuaia? Never heard of it.'

'It's a town in Tierra del Fuego, an archipelago at the very bottom of the country.'

Cliff had heard the name Tierra del Fuego before, but knew nothing of it. 'Why would he go there?'

'I have an idea,' replied Alejo, stroking his chin and looking directly at Cliff. He was obviously having fun and wasn't going to let himself be rushed. 'But,' he eventually continued, 'according to our records, Ushuaia wasn't his only destination over the years.'

Cliff decided to play along. After all, he'd know everything that Alejo did within the next half hour. He had chided Roy enough about his impatience, now it was time for him to practise what he preached. 'Really? Where else did he go?'

'Every other time he was here, he was registered in a hotel in Gaiman.'

'Gaiman?' Cliff looked flummoxed. 'I'm sorry Alejo. I must seem rude but I've never heard of that place either.'

'To be honest, neither had I my sweet man,' laughed Alejo, who for a second went off topic and gave Cliff's inner thigh a gentle squeeze. Cliff put his own hand on top of Alejo's and left it there. At the same time, his eyes urged Alejo to continue. 'Gaiman is a small town in the Chubut province of Patagonia.'

Cliff grew more excited and was now firmly holding Alejo's hand. 'Patagonia. Doesn't it have ties with Wales?'

'Yes, and Germany too,' replied Alejo. 'Lots of people from both countries settled there. I think that began for the Welsh migrants in the mid to late 19th century'.

'James Paisley was Scottish, born of Northern Irish Protestant stock.'

'Stock?' Alejo interrupted. 'I've never heard that turn of phrase. Were they seen as inferior animals?'

'Of course not,' answered Cliff, not minding his thoughts being diverted. 'It's just another way of describing our heritage. We are animals as well, I suppose, but you are right. It does sound a bit derogatory.'

'As I was saying, before being interrupted,' he stopped to give Alejo a kiss on the lips to show he was only teasing, 'we have no link between Paisley and Wales. I suppose Hereford, where he trained, has a border, but that is tenuous and takes us no further.' Alejo took a sip of his coffee, enjoying, if not fully understanding, Cliff's stream of consciousness. 'We will need to look at Paisley's army records again. But what about this place, Oosh…' He paused, looking at Alejo for help.

'Ushuaia.'

'Yes, Ushuaia. Why go there?'

'Well, this is where my second bit of research may help,' he paused, enjoying the moment of power he was holding over his lover. 'We know Paisley was part of the task force sent down to steal the Malvinas back from us.' He was grinning as he said this, but deep down he was still appalled by the British occupation of the islands. They had avoided the topic so far and he didn't want to start an argument, which might cause irreparable damage to their burgeoning relationship, so he quickly moved on. 'During that conflict, Ushuaia was a key component in our fight.'

'How so?' Cliff asked.

'Well, we have a large naval base there. The Admiral Berisso Integrated Naval Base, I think is how you call it in the UK, was the port for much of our fleet and aircraft. It was also the disembarkation point for our ground troops too.'

Cliff mulled this over but couldn't see what importance it had in their investigation. 'Yes, I get that. I see a geographical link to the time Paisley was serving here. But …'

Alejo held up his hand to stop Cliff from saying any more. 'What you aren't considering my friend is that our resentment towards the UK over las Malvinas goes back way before 1982. That has been a real bone of contention since you claimed sovereignty. Openly, we may have been quiet and inert towards your Government, but we have always tried to undermine your position.' Cliff was listening intently. He knew Alejo was about to drop a bombshell and he wanted to fully understand it. 'I had heard stories of us trying to destabilise your country, but until my research this morning I had never seen a concrete example. Ushuaia is also the training ground for our special troops. Just like Hereford for your SAS and San Diego for the Navy Seals. We too perpetrate black operations. Secret covert campaigns, which are signed off by only the most senior government officials, and run out of Ushuaia. Well one such campaign was funding the IRA.'

'That could be the link.' Cliff's voice was raised in excitement. 'But what do you mean by "funded"?'

'We would never admit to it, but we are, in relative terms to many Western countries, quite poor. Even so, for such an important target we would routinely, throughout the troubles, send the IRA money. When I say money, I mean gold.'

'And the gold was stored in Tierra del Fuego.' Cliff decided to avoid further embarrassment by not having to try to pronounce 'Ushuaia' again.

'It was a natural location. Away from prying eyes and guarded by our elite troops. However, that operation was shut down during the war. No clear reason was given, but then it wasn't in the public domain anyway. Whether it was a coincidence or not, there was a spate of demotions of rank for many of the hierarchy at the base. Even rumours of court-martials being held, which wouldn't be normal during such an active time militarily.

'So,' Cliff was trying to piece all of this together, 'we know Paisley was independently wealthy living as Paddy Cullen. How did he get that wealth?' He looked at his watch. It was already 10pm in Britain. On a Friday night, who knows where Chas and Roy would be. Knowing he needed a 3-way group chat, he sent a WhatsApp message to organise a call for noon the following day, Buenos Aries time. Having done that, he turned back to Alejo and explained what he had just done.

'I need the guys to find out about Paisley's link to Wales and whether he was sent to Tierra del Fuego during the war. Could he have found and stolen the gold?' Cliff sounded doubtful.

'I agree,' replied Alejo. 'At the moment there is some circumstantial evidence that makes it a possibility, but did he have the opportunity to do so? Otherwise it is just a fanciful possibility

'Maybe our chat tomorrow will shed more light on the matter? I don't know how to thank you.'

'Alejo partially filled two glasses from the brandy decanter behind him, and passed one of them to Cliff. His free hand then helped Cliff to his feet. 'I'm sure I can think of something.' With that he turned towards the master bedroom.

Chapter 15

Dana looked at Chas as he was shutting down his laptop. He was so deliberate and careful. Qualities that she knew could infuriate others, but, watching him wait for the screen to go black before finally closing the lid and turning the power off at the wall socket, her heart was bursting with love for the man. Never had she felt unsupported, neglected or bored. In fact, it was totally the opposite. What some ill-informed people might take for dull, was merely a façade. A façade that masked the hidden depths of an interesting, passionate and caring man. They had, in her mind, a perfect relationship where they balanced their time between mutual pursuits, such as gardening where they were together, and their own individual hobbies: sports and poker for Chas, and Pilates and art for Dana. Dana had never had cause to look elsewhere. Even in the bedroom Chas had always been attentive and adventurous. Something which would have surprised others such as Roy and Cliff. When Chas mentioned his toys cupboard, they thought it was full of board games or a packed away train set. Little did they know or suspect what was really in it.

'Did you send it then?' Dana asked.

'Yes, decided my message was a little long for WhatsApp, so emailed a short summary of my Hereford trip to them. My mobile is on charge in the office anyway.'

Dana handed Chas a small glass of whisky and took a sip of her own Bailey's. They weren't big drinkers, by any standards, but during lockdown they had got into the habit of a small alcoholic drink 'to take the edge off' and help them sleep during what was, without doubt, a scary time. Sitting on their individual recliner chairs, drinks to the outside and holding hands across the two inner arms of the chairs, it was the perfect end to another day.

Had the curtains not been drawn, they would have seen the danger reflected in the window. That would have probably only added increased fear or panic, because the assault was so swift that they wouldn't have been able to react. The choreographed strike meant that they were simultaneously attacked. Chas felt himself being grabbed from behind, with an immensely strong forearm pulling him back. The quick transfer in weight caused the chair to tip backwards, with Chas' torso now parallel to the floor and his legs rather pointlessly flailing in the air. He glimpsed his masked assailant, dressed from top to toe in black, nimbly spring over the chair, landing on Chas' stomach. Without pause the attacker started to punch Chas in the body and face. Chas, who had been severely winded, couldn't yell out as he felt heavy blows rain down on him. The rat-a-tat punching was so aggressive and swift that Chas couldn't even identify which part of the body or face was being struck. That was not the case when his genitals received two of the blows. That pain, as any man will attest, is unique and long-lasting.

Chas was helpless to defend himself, but he had to know what was happening to Dana. From his prone position, he could, through a squinting left-eye see Dana being hoisted one-armed over her chair. He saw his brave wife then receive three punches across her face, as she tried to wriggle free, making to bite the second assailant's arm as she squirmed. Once the other man, dressed in the same fashion, had got her over the chair he pressed his knees on top of her to hold her there. As Chas watched the man zip tie her hands and then ankles, he felt the same being done to him.

'Gag her, and take her upstairs,' said the man who had attacked Chas. 'Do with her what you want. When I get what we need from this old git, then you can stop.' Even through the mask, Chas knew the man was affecting and changing his voice. Why? Did he have a distinctive accent, or even worse, did Chas know him? Whatever the truth was, Chas needed to do what was required to make sure Dana, and he for that matter, survived. As hopeless as it seemed, he had to believe there was a way out of this. Dana was now slung over her attacker's shoulders and being taken, head first, to the staircase.

'Right then,' his attacker started, having plopped Chas, as if he were a small sack of potatoes, onto Dana's chair, 'you and me have some talking to do.' With that, he hit Chas twice. These punches hurt Chas much more as both of them were static and he could swing freer. 'This man you see, stole something from us. And we want it back.' He started to unfold a piece of paper. As Chas was trying to make the image out, he was distracted by some muffled yells coming from upstairs.

'Dana! What is the bastard doing to you?' he worried.

His attention went back to the piece of paper, but his slowness in responding had obviously angered his assailant, because three more blows came in. This time to the chest.

'Come on you old bastard. He's a big boy, my mate. And he likes it rough.' As if on cue, more muffled cries worked their way down the stairs.

'Focus!' Chas told himself. Through what were surely now badly bruised eyes, he recognised it as being the front page of the Daventry Express. The one reporting the murder of Paddy Cullen. On it, half of the page was taken up by a picture of Paddy receiving a trophy at a bowls awards ceremony. His attacker must have seen a look of recognition spread across his face, as a close up punch hit him once more. Square on the nose. 'So, you do know him. Tell me everything.'

Chas could hear more muffled screams and bangs coming from what he presumed was their bedroom. He could hardly recognise his own voice as he said. 'Tell him to stop, please.'

The response wasn't what Chas had expected. Instead of him calling out, he hit him once more. 'You start talking first.' So he did. True to his word the man went to the hallway and called upstairs. Immediately, all sounds up there stopped.

Every fact Chas gave was checked and rechecked, and then follow up questions were asked. Eventually, the man seemed satisfied. He called up to his friend and they left as silently as they arrived, turning all the lights in the house off.

Chas had told them almost everything they knew, including the tattoos on the body, probably details of a Swiss bank account. He said they didn't have access to the tattoo. They had never seen it. They only knew about it because they knew someone in the police, who had given them a few facts from the coroner's report. He also told them where Paddy had lived. The one thing he didn't tell them was what Cliff and Roy were doing now. He told them he was Paddy's best friend, and it was his idea to find out the truth.

As he lay there in the dark, he strained to hear a noise from above. This time he wanted to hear something. It would show that Dana was still alive. 'Please God, let her be alive. Let her be ok.' Chas heard nothing and started to sob. He continued to do so until his body gave in to the pain, and darkness fell over him.

Chapter 16

Roy looked around the breakfast table. The Kelly's were chatting away, oblivious to his thoughts. 'How could one family, strangers only a few weeks ago, selflessly do so much for one person in such a short time?' He looked at Michael, carefully buttering his toast, unable to believe how brave he had been the day before.

They had been in Seamus' car lost in a conversation over Roy's preference for flat racing over the jumps, when they both noticed a man, casually dressed and wearing a blue baseball cap, pulled right down to his eyes, stepping off the pavement in front of the car. Roy, more intent on winning the argument, thought nothing of it until

Michael yelled, 'Get down!', while at the same time pulling Roy down onto his own legs. As Roy's head moved, he could see the man's right hand reach for the back of his belt. Roy saw no more, because as soon as his head hit Michael's lap, he felt a weight across his shoulders. Michael had lain on top of Roy in order to protect him.

From Roy's perspective, what then ensued was a sporadic and disparate set of sounds, including voices, which he could just about make out over his own heavy breathing. Michael, who could only see a little better through the windscreen, as he too was seeking cover on the back seat, filled in the gaps for Roy later.

Michael explained that the man had indeed produced a pistol from either his belt or a holster secreted around the back of his trousers. As he was bringing it up to point at them, he was distracted by Seamus and Declan rushing out of the café, calling out to the gunman. Knowing that all police in Northern Ireland are armed, he turned and ran up the narrow alley beside the car, which meant that he kept the vehicle between him and Declan, who by now had drawn his weapon and was calling for backup on his Airwave. Telling Seamus to wait by the car and keep the older men safe, Declan cautiously pursued the attacker staying close to the rubbish skips, which neighbouring establishments kept there. He arrived at the far end of the alley to see a black BMW 3 Series speeding off down the road. Given the little lead the assailant had had, Declan concluded that he must have had an accomplice waiting for him in the car. Declan couldn't get the full licence plate, but he was sure it contained the letter combination, AZ. A letter sequence giving the car its origin, Belfast.

Having dropped Michael and Roy off at the pub, Seamus had, on Declan's request, gone to the police station. Because he had had a good look at the two suspects, the previous evening, they wanted Seamus to trawl through their photo album of mugshots. By the time he got there, things had already moved on. Clearly realising the car was being hunted, the two men had already gone to a waste area near the River Foyle and set the BMW on fire, thereby destroying any forensic evidence. 'They will have had a clean car already there waiting for them,' explained Declan. 'They needed a fast car to get away, irrespective of whether the hit had been successful or not. They are probably now in a Hyundai or Kia on back roads in the Republic. Something innocuous anyway.' Declan couldn't hide his frustration.

With a strong cup of coffee, Seamus had spent forty minutes perusing the seemingly inexhaustible number of mugshots, not in an album like in the films but projected from a computer database onto a large screen they had erected in an interview room. He had been told that the database had already been filtered to show men, between the ages of 25 and 45, and included both criminals and known associates of terrorist organisations. Ironically, since the Good Friday Agreement it had been difficult to distinguish between the two, particularly when it came to organised crime.

Finally, Declan made a positive identification, Micky O'Donovan. He was the large guy with cropped hair, bushy beard and scar above his right eye. Once that he had found the first suspect, the female officer beside him typed something into the computer and six more mugshots appeared on the large screen.

'These are his known associates,' she clarified.

Apparently, the suspected getaway driver was called Thomas Ahern. Well, that was the guy who Seamus identified as being with O'Donovan in the pub the previous evening.

'For feck's sake,' laughed Michael, when he was told the names by Seamus. 'Who'd be giving such a saintly name like Michael to a scumbag like that.' Those around him in the pub laughed as well. Some of that merriment stemmed from relief. Relief that their old friend was safe. News travelled quickly around Kellys and the neighbourhood. Especially news like that. He then spoke quietly to Roy, who was on his second Guinness. 'O'Donovan? That can't be a coincidence.'

For the rest of that day, either Michael or Seamus remained with Roy. Even when he went for a pee, one of them stopped anyone they didn't know well or trust from going into the toilet after him. Roy, for his part, was not particularly scared. Back in Daventry maybe, but in Derry, with the Kellys, he seemed so protected. The fact that four bets he placed all won, even a 33-1 outsider, kept his spirits high. The hero, Michael, on the other hand had a lean time of it, winning only once when a favourite romped home. He had scoffed at Roy's choice of the outsider saying 'that one's only good for the glue factory'. When it pipped Michael's choice at the finishing post, he pointed at Roy, using his finger to mimic a pistol and declared. 'Should have let the bastard shoot you.' With that the two, both now slightly the worse for wear, fell roaring with laughter into each other's arms.

Michael, buttered toast in hand, turned to Roy. 'Eat up, the game starts at 11.00am'

'Game?' Roy asked.

'Yes, Saturday morning means GAA time. And you have one last meeting.'

'Here we go again,' thought Roy, but said instead. 'In your vernacular, 'what the feck is GAA?'

The Kellys, as is their wont when it comes to Roy, didn't reply. They just laughed.

....

Roy had never worn another man's thermals before. He had, of course, worn Mrs Grimble no. 2's silk undies on occasion, but had flatly refused a request to don her thong. 'The back strap could cut me in half like it were a guillotine, and my two veg would be hanging out either side at the front, like Dumbo's ears,' he had protested. Siobhan, Michael's wife, had insisted he needed them. 'You'd be catching yer death there without dem,' she had argued.

Reluctantly, he had taken Michael's winter unmentionables from her and put them on. Having decided that sniffing them might not help, maybe only make him a little queasy if there were indeed a questionable odour, he decided to wear them over his own boxers. 'He's a nice man, and saved my life, but I don't really want my bits rubbing up against where his bits have regularly been.' This was his irrational logic, because he'd actually seen Siobhan take them out of the tumble dryer. With his trousers on top, that made three layers to work through should he need a wee. 'Bloody hell,' was his next thought and worry, 'if it's that cold I don't know if it will be long enough to poke out, having negotiated all of that.'

Standing there on the sideline of the Gaelic football pitch, wishing he had borrowed some gloves too, he gave a silent thanks to Siobhan. She had been right, because all around him he could see men stamping their feet, or blowing into their hands, in an attempt not to freeze to death. To his side, Michael was cheering for his team the Shamrocks, not surprisingly, wearing the green and white hoops of Celtic, in the local derby match with Balinderry, who sported a more somber coloured kit, red with black piping. Michael hadn't spoken to Roy since five minutes after the kick off when Roy's fourth inane comment finally got on Michael's nerves. He had either corrected Roy, or just smiled to the first three. 'It's not really football, more like tag with the odd kick.' 'The goalie doesn't do much does he?' 'This four step rule looks stupid. Why do they have different options?' However, when Roy stated, 'Really, they catch a ball and for that everyone has to back off and let him kick for goal. And he doesn't even have to beat the keeper. Not very skilful hoofing it between that wide target.' Michael wanted to respond. 'Thought you were a prize winning journalist.' Instead, he turned away from Michael, his ignorance tolerance had been breached.

Fortunately for Roy, the Shamrocks were on top right from the start. So, with five minutes to go before halftime, he turned back to his annoying, but somehow still likeable and easy to forgive, English friend. 'Right, we are meeting him at halftime inside the drinks pavilion,' he explained pointing at a temporary marquee, which had been erected that morning just for the match.

Roy, knowing he had been given a reprieve, had a thousand questions he wanted to ask, but for once common sense kicked in, and he settled on. 'Who is it that I'm going to meet?'

'His name is Gerry Collins, and during the late 1970's, when Padraig O'Toole was in Derry, he was a member of the IRA and on the Army Council.' Before Roy could seek clarification with a follow up question, Michael added. 'That means he was near the very top of the IRA hierarchy. He was a decision maker, and as such knew virtually everything that was going on.'

In the drinks pavilion, Roy wasn't so much drinking his hot chocolate, but holding onto it, in the hope that his hands would thaw out and spring back to life. Sitting low down at a table with Michael, he could only see a wall of other men who had also sought a break from the icy wind outside. All of a sudden, there was an almost biblical separation in the wall of people and a large individual in his thirties appeared. Behind him, almost comically, followed an elderly man, virtually half his size. The reverence paid to this man, by many of the others there, told Roy that this was Gerry Collins. They say size doesn't matter. Little people can do big things, scary things, atrocious things. Roy realised that this diminutive balding man, with a kind face and friendly blue eyes, had 'for the cause' sanctioned the deaths of many people. Maybe, he had cut his own teeth carrying out some heinous acts. Of course, Gerry would have seen his actions and decisions as being justified, necessary and part of their fight for freedom.

Michael introduced Gerry to Roy, who stood up and shook his hand. When everyone was seated, Gerry spoke. 'Now my dear old friend Michael has explained your situation. And before this chat goes any further I want to assure you we had nothing to do with the bombing a few weeks ago. Nor did we sanction it. In fact, we condemn those who did. She was a good journalist, which made her slightly annoying for us at times. But she was always fair and unbiased.' Roy wasn't sure how to respond to this, but any embarrassment Roy was starting to feel disappeared when Gerry continued. 'Now let me tell you what I know about O'Toole.'

By the time Gerry had finished, the second half had started meaning that the tent was all but empty. Roy had listened closely, and, because of the lack of anything new or useful, he hadn't needed to interrupt or pose any questions. Gerry was still seething that their security had been breached with O'Toole gaining their trust. Like 'a fecking weasel', Gerry's words, he had skulked away just before the dawn raid and had never been seen again. Gerry said that he was still on their 'hit list', saying 'there are some things the Good Friday Agreement can't absolve.' He condemned O'Toole for the deaths of his two loyal soldiers, Mary and Brian, and added 'Of course, in a sense, he did for the wee ones too. They were found on a relative's doorstep and spirited away from the mess. Not long after, we heard that one or both had tragically died. A right bastard that O'Toole was.'

Sensing Gerry had finished, Roy thanked him, adding. Well, you can rest assured that the man you knew as O'Toole is dead. Murdered. His real name was James Paisley and lived in our community as Paddy Cullen.' Roy sighed. 'I think we have found out everything we can from his time here. I hope our investigation in Argentina can move us further along.'

Gerry leant forward. '

Argentina, you say. We used to get funding from them until it suddenly stopped in 1982. It wasn't much but we certainly missed it when it was gone.'

'Would O'Toole have known that?' Roy asked, suddenly now more interested.

'It was an open secret, I suppose,' replied Gerry. 'Just like the money that was sent from Boston. The gold used to arrive moulded hidden in crockery sets as teapots, dishes and forks. It was a joke you see, because it was shipped from Tierra del Fuego. TDF, teapots, dishes and forks. Yes,' he added, 'O'Toole would have known that.'

Roy thanked Gerry once more. This time with greater enthusiasm.

'Come on Michael. We've a game to watch.'

Chapter 17

Roy was sitting in the bar at Kellys, nursing a pint of Guinness 0%. Although he could handle a drink in the evening, starting on alcohol at lunchtime was fatal, with him often falling asleep. He knew he needed to have his full wits about him for the important call that was to come. As he watched Michael down his second undiluted pint in celebration of the thrashing handed out by the Shamrocks, Roy was cursing Cliff for arranging the group WhatsApp call for a time that suited him in Argentina. 'I bet him and his mate have been at it like rabbits all night, and all morning, only stopping for breakfast,' he taunted himself with this image. 'While I freeze my bollocks off, and get to chat with the IRA equivalent of the Godfather.'

'Any racing on?' Roy asked, picking up a copy of the Racing Post from the table in front of him.

'Is the Pope a Catholic?' Michael laughed. 'Now if you had said that, I'd have called you out for blasphemy.' Not sure if his argument made sense, he picked up the remote control to change the channel from the Motor GP in Portugal, to the final races at Newbury. 'Only a novice hurdle and a bumper left,' he commented. 'But beggars can't be choosers.'

Having had no luck between them this time, Roy made sure he was upstairs and near the flat's rather ancient router by 4.55pm. Siobhan brought him a nice sweet hot cup of tea, which reminded Roy that he was still wearing Michael's thermals. He quickly nipped to his room to take them off before the call. To his surprise his undercarriage suddenly felt liberated. It felt so airy down there, he needed to check his fly to ensure he wouldn't be exposing himself to Michael's wife. 'There is only so much excitement a woman can take.'

Roy knew that Cliff would make the call on the dot of 5pm. What amazed them both was the absence of Chas. Of the three, he was always the most dependable.

'Did he see the message?' Roy asked.

'Don't know,' replied Cliff. 'What with the time difference and everything that has been going on, I didn't check.'

'Really,' said Roy. His voice now full of smuttiness and innuendo. 'And what precisely has been going on? You do look a bit peaky. Or have you got that bloody sepia filter on?' Roy started laughing. Now and then, he amazed himself with his lightning sharp wit.

'Bloody cheek! Peaky,' chortled Cliff in reply. 'Now, a gentleman never tells, but my activities have certainly not been on the peaky side.'

'If I'm not going to get any details,' said Roy, a bit deflated by his friend's reticence, 'can you at least tell me if you've taken any of my special pills.'

Cliff's face reddened. 'Almost run out actually.' Roy had never seen Cliff look so coy.

'Glad you've had some fun, mate. You deserve it. What's Buenos Aries like?'

Cliff, who had fallen in love, maybe not only with Buenos Aries, answered at length describing everything in detail. Roy had never visited South America, so he listened enviously until Cliff, in mid description of the cemetery, changed the topic. 'It's almost 5.20. Where is Chas?' He was starting to get concerned.

'Let's share what we have found out,' suggested Roy, 'and then you can chase him up. See whether he got the message et cetera.'

Cliff went first, telling Roy about Paisley's trips to Argentina, mentioning Ushuaia, and Patagonia. When he explained that Ushuaia was in Tierra del Fuego, Roy interrupted and told of his meeting with Gerry Collins and the smuggled gold in the form of kitchenware. Cliff couldn't believe how their two totally separate investigations had confirmed links between Paisley and Tierra del Fuego.

'Because he had wormed his way into the Derry Brigade of the IRA,' said Roy, 'he knew how the gold got there. And where it came from.'

'So, if he somehow found out where the gold was stored, then he could have stolen it at source,' added Cliff, following Roy's line of thought.

'That's' a big 'if',' mused Roy.

'He would have had to have hidden it somewhere down there,' continued Cliff. 'Even a small amount of gold is heavy and hard to conceal. In a makeshift temporary military camp even more so.'

'He must have been playing the long game,' said Roy. 'Waiting for the war to end, and then bringing it back…'

'In small quantities,' interrupted Cliff. His voice now quite excited. 'That's why he went there so often.'

'But he quickly stopped going to Ushuaia. He must have transferred it to Patagonia.'

'Agreed,' replied Cliff, 'but what is his link to Patagonia? There is nothing Welsh about him or his life.'

'Nothing we've found yet, anyway.'

That part of the investigation exhausted, Cliff asked. 'Did you find out anything else?'

He shook his head in disbelief and sadness, as Roy described the plight of the O'Donovan twins. He was even more outraged and upset when Roy told him of the attempt on his life, and the courageous acts of the Kellys.

'He sounds a great guy, this Michael,' said Cliff.

'He is,' replied Roy. 'In fact, they all are.'

The talk of the attempt on Roy's life reminded Cliff of the absence of Chas in the call.

'Right, let's end the call now. I need to find out what's going on with Chas.'

'Good idea,' replied Roy. 'Let me know what you find out.'

Cliff finished the call and searched for his text to Chas. It had two grey ticks signifying that Chas' phone had received the message. However, they weren't blue, showing that he hadn't read it. Now getting quite worried he tried WhatsApp calling Chas. No reply.

'To hell with the cost,' he thought, and rang Chas' landline. It went straight to BT voicemail. He then tried to call his daughter, Samantha, on WhatsApp. She didn't pick up either. Cliff felt so far out of the loop and impotent. Reluctantly, he resorted to messaging her. '*Can you check on Chas? I can't get hold of him, and I'm starting to worry, Thanks luv*'.

There was nothing else he could do. Just wait.

Chapter 18

Samantha Doyle was lying face down diagonally across her half of the king-size bed. Her right arm was visible, outstretched reaching past her pillow. While her legs, slightly bent at the knee, were hidden under the crumpled duvet, which only covered her side of the bed.

Her partner Adam entered the room with a wry smile on his face and a breakfast tray in his hands.

'No wonder I woke up freezing,' he thought, looking down at his own naked body. 'If she doesn't stop doing this, I'm going to need some thermal pyjamas.'

He set the tray down on the night table on his side of the bed, and leant across, pulling a wayward strand of her mahogany hair to the side so that it exposed her ear. Kneeling now on the bed, his lips went to the ear, and he whispered her name in a way that she would feel the words from his breath as much as hear them. Samantha reacted by extending her neck, like she was trying to get her ear away from the gentle puff of air. Almost simultaneously, she opened her eyes, just enough to locate the source of the irritation. Seeing Adam smiling down at her, she couldn't help but return the gesture.

'Good morning,' she said, with a yawn as her left arm stretched out from under the quilt to join its mirror twin.

Adam sensing a moment of vulnerability suddenly straddled her, and, pinning her arms where they were, began to sensually nibble her long neck. 'Good morning,' he replied. 'Last night was sensational.'

'This morning will be too. But first,' she countered, bringing her legs up to ease him off, 'I need a cup of tea and some toast.' Her eyes had spied the tray behind Adam. And nothing stopped this police officer from getting her man, or in this case, her breakfast.

They were, to the outsider, the perfect couple. Each being naturally fit and good looking, they could have easily been people you would hate just for being so lucky. But they were kind and good people, both serving the community. Sam in her job, kept criminals off the street, and Fireman Adam rescued people when in trouble. They had been together almost five years, buying the new build in Monksmoor on Daventry's northern outskirts once they knew they were meant to be together. However, the perceived perfect couple started to drift apart. Obviously, the stress and strain of day-to-day living took its toll, but it was the shift-work nature of both their jobs, which meant they spent very little time with each other. One day, Adam came home and told Sam that he had almost strayed. He was in tears, hating himself, but he had been wise enough to resist temptation and tell his partner. They each took a day's leave to allow themselves to get away together to the coast, and talk things through. DI Bridges, Sam's immediate superior, wasn't best pleased at the time as Sam was involved in a major drug investigation. However, when Sam confided in Cliff about this, he used the fact that he and Bridges were both members at Staverton Golf Club to intervene on Sam's behalf. The DI duly relented. The outcome of that pow-wow by the sea was a monthly break, either at home or away. They would take it in turns to use pieces of their annual holiday allowance, and shut themselves off from the outside world. Apart from collecting takeaways and maybe a drink at the odd pub, that would be the same even if they remained in Daventry. They were midway through one such home-break.

'Hold on,' laughed Adam, righting himself and holding Samantha back. 'I've made enough for two. Don't be a pig.' With that he started to kiss her neck. By the time they had finished rolling around, both the toast and the tea were stone cold.

'I suppose at least there's no crumbs in the bed,' said Sam. With that she extravagantly threw the duvet, which by now was on the floor, over them both and fitted her body up against Adam, like naked spoons.

....

It was dark outside when they eventually woke up.

'I'm hungry,' moaned Adam. 'Shall we order an Indian?'

'Good idea,' replied Sam, surprised that she was on Adam's side of the bed. She reached out to turn on the bedside lamp, but, in the darkness, pushed the breakfast tray instead. Immediately after they heard the noise of something, or things, hitting the floor.

'What the hell was that?' Adam said, sitting up.

'Don't know,' replied Sam, now reaching a little higher to find the lamp switch, and not the tray again. This time the light went on, and Sam leaned out of the bed, trying to see what had caused the noise. 'Bugger!'

'What is it?' Adam was sounding a little worried.

'Our bloody phones fell on the floor. You must have put the tray right next to them.'

She sprung out of bed. 'Hope the screens haven't cracked.' She bent down and picked up the two phones. Without checking, she handed Adam his mobile, and then pushed the button to illuminate her iPhone.

'I've missed two calls and four messages from dad.' Although her voice conveyed her concern, the dexterity of her fingers showed she was in full control. Adam just watched and waited.

'Fancy a roundabout route to the takeaway?' she asked, starting to gather her clothes together from the floor.

'What's going on?' Adam was pushing back the duvet, also scanning the floor for what he was going to put on

'Dad's worried about Chas. He wants us to check in on him.'

....

As Sam approached the front door, she became immediately concerned as there wasn't a light to be seen in the house. Through her father, she had become more than an acquaintance with Chas and Dana over the past few years. Knowing Cliff's inability to decline a glass of red wine, or a final more alcoholic digestif, she had often acted as chauffeur for the group. Reciprocally, Chas and Dana had invited her and Adam to the occasional dinner party. In all of the times she had picked them up from the house, she had always been aware that the ever cautious Chas left at least one light on. Presumably, to deter any potential burglar.

With a slightly impatient, and definitely hungry, Adam waiting in the car out on the road, she rang the bell. Nothing. She went to the living room window, but the curtains were drawn. Back at the door she opened the letter box and called their names. With the wind blowing, she wasn't sure whether she heard something in reply. Getting increasingly concerned, she circled around to the back of the house. All of the windows were shut, and apart from the kitchen window, the curtains were all pulled.

'Bloody energy costs,' she thought, knowing that everyone was doing this to save money during the winter time. And Chas being Chas, was more careful than most.

She took out her phone and switched on the torch application, shining it through the kitchen window. Nothing untoward. Just Dana's immaculately equipped kitchen looking so clean that it might have never been used. Keeping the torch on, she pointed it at the back door. As she went to pull the handle, in the vain hope it might be open, she noticed a little damage to the wood next to the lock. It had been forced, probably jimmied. Now she wasn't surprised that it opened. Deciding time was of the essence, she went in carefully not touching anything. Not even a light switch.

Knowing the layout from her previous visits there, she made her way to the living room, thanking the inventors of smartphones for including such a useful tool as the torch. Although not providing a particularly strong beam, it did illuminate the surrounding space well enough to navigate without a problem. She did a double take as she entered the room. Initially, she blamed the weird shadows cast by the torch for making it look like a chair had been tipped over. But then the reality kicked in and she accepted it as fact. Turning the torch to the right she saw the body of Chas, head lulling to one side. She needed better light, so she carefully pushed the light switch at a point not normally touched. Even though the torch app was now unnecessary, as the room was suddenly filled with light, she left it on, more concerned for the life of her father's best friend than the life of the phone's battery. She could see him clearly. He was lying limp in an unnatural position, his head battered and bloody. As she ran to approach him from the front she saw a wet patch in the crotch of his trousers. Even as she was searching for a pulse, she had the irrational thought of how unhappy Chas would be to have been found in such an undignified way. And by a female to boot. She almost cried with joy as she felt a slight pulse in his neck.

'Chas. It's me, Sam,' she said, more in hope than anything else.

Chas let out a small sigh, almost a sob, forcing his eyes to open a little bit.

'Chas, thank God! You'll be fine. Dana? Do you know where Dana is?' He didn't seem able to reply, but with an almighty effort, he tilted his head to the left and his eyes looked towards the hallway.

'Is she upstairs?' Sam urged, following his gaze. He blinked once, as a tear formed in the corner of that eye. 'Don't worry. I'll find her.'

With that she speed dialled Adam, opening the front door as she did so. 'Call an ambulance and get the police here. Then get in here and bring the emergency first aid bag with you.'

Not waiting for a reply she ran up the stairs, again trying not to touch the bannister. The torch app was once more doing its job well. In the master bedroom she found a partially clothed, but conscious Dana, mouth muzzled with ankles and wrists zip tied together. The latter also being fastened around one of the bed's four posts.

Sam removed the ball of wool from her mouth. It had been used to silence her. Then as she cut the zip ties she said reassuringly. 'Chas is going to be ok. We've got help coming.'

'I don't want to be seen like this,' cried Dana, looking down at the ripped cotton panties around her ankles and urine stained duvet. With her hands now freed, she made to pull her panties up. Sam, despite the fact that she was sensitive to how vulnerable and embarrassed this elderly lady must feel, put an arm out to prevent Dana from doing so.

'We need to preserve any DNA,' she said, softly. 'We will need any evidence we can get to nail these animals. Don't worry, it will only be you me and a female Scene of Crime Officer. Wait here, my sweet.' Dana, who was still sobbing, nodded.

Sam then swiftly ran downstairs past the living room, where Adam was helping Chas the best he could, and into the kitchen. She grabbed a box of freezer bags and ran back upstairs to Dana, only stopping to pick up a duvet off the single bed in the spare room. Dana was as she had left her. She carefully teased the panties off Dana and into one of the freezer bags. Finally she guided Dana into her sewing chair, which was set in the alcove of the bay window. Placing the duvet around her she said. 'Right, let's get you a hot sweet cup of tea.'

In the kitchen, while the kettle was boiling, she made two phone calls. The first was to her friend, Tina, a SOCO. She knew her to be sensitive and full of integrity. Sam wanted her to be the one to examine Dana. Secondly, she called her father Cliff. Although it wasn't good news, he needed to be told. At least they were both alive.

Now all she could do was wait with Dana. Until help arrived

Chapter 19

Samantha turned into Chas and Dana's drive and stopped next to Chas' silver Kia Sportage. She hadn't slept a wink since waking up in Adam's arms the previous afternoon. Caffeine and anger were driving her. She knew she would have to succumb to rest later, but for now she was as alert as ever.

As she shut the car door, she saw PC Angela Chalmers, a trained victim support officer, standing in the porch. Dana had insisted on staying in the house. 'Alex and Shelley have taken the kids to Lapland to see Father Christmas,' she had explained, when Dana had suggested informing her son, thinking it might be best to spend the night somewhere else. 'Hugh and Zoe have been so much looking forward to it. Neither of us would want to interrupt their special trip. They'll be home on Tuesday anyway.'

When the first ambulance arrived, the focus had been on Chas. Despite her protestations, Dana had been convinced to remain upstairs.

'We need you to be examined. Here is better,' said Sam. 'If you aren't in need of hospitalisation, then we can get you showered and changed. That'll be the Dana that Chas wants to see.' Dana still wasn't sure, but relented when Sam told her Adam would follow behind in the ambulance.

Literally, as the first ambulance left to take Chas to hospital, a second one arrived. By that time, Tina Okofor, the SOCO officer was starting to process the room. She knew that Dana's health needed to be checked first before she could look at Dana herself.

'God bless the NHS,' thought Sam, as, Darren, the male paramedic, had absented himself. Having checked that her vital signs were stable and that she was in full control of her faculties, which thankfully Dana was, Darren had realised the sensitive nature of the situation. There were enough qualified women there to perform the more delicate examinations without needing him present.

Sam kept herself at a reasonable distance, with her eyes averted, while Tina and Stacey, the female paramedic, calmly and professionally went about their jobs. Stacey had wonderful interpersonal skills, preparing Dana for each step, while Tina gently took swab samples.

'There are some contusions and bruising on your face, neck and chest,' observed Tina, taking photos of the injuries.

'I think that was when he grabbed me out of the chair,' replied Dana, still in shock, but visibly more composed. 'Also,' she added, feeling the crown of her head, amongst her short auburn hair, 'I hit my head against the wall when he was carrying me upstairs.'

Tina's voice softened. 'You have some vaginal bruising. Did he penetrate you?'

'I don't think so.' Dana started to sob, as she forced herself to relive the scene. 'He started to undo his trousers and took out his penis. But, I don't think he was capable of more.'

Sam didn't want to ask, but she had to. 'So, why are you bruised there?'

Dana looked towards the floor under the window. 'He used that,' she wailed. 'He teased me with it, and then started to push it in me.'

Sam followed her gaze, and saw a large red candle lying there. She looked at the small crafting table next to it. On it there were five or six other candles and some wrapping paper. 'The bastard,' thought Sam. 'She was making them as Christmas gifts, and he used it to abuse her.'

'I think I was lucky,' continued Dana. 'Just as he did that, his friend called for them to go.'

'I will need to take a swab sample anyway. Just in case,' said Tina, her voice not hiding the emotion and anger she was also feeling.

Once the examination was finished, Dana asked Sam to keep her word. So, having found some clothes while Dana was showering, she drove her to the hospital.

Dana, who was used to what is normally perceived as a disconcerting environment because of her volunteering at the local hospice, seemed to relax when she saw Chas through the window of his ward. It was a ward set up with four beds, but amazingly the other three were unoccupied. Sam was surprised by her reaction because he looked in a worse state than she remembered. 'Are you Ok?' Sam whispered to Dana, as they approached his bed.

'Not really. But this is the best place for him,' she replied. 'He can heal here. He is a strong man.' Sam felt a little inadequate beside this immensely strong woman. She began to wonder whether her love ran as deep for Adam.

Chas' eyes were shut, but his chest was moving reassuringly up and down in a strong rhythm.

Dana sat in the chair next to the bed, and started to soothingly stroke his hand.

'I'm here love. Don't you be fretting about me.' She was leaning in to kiss his cheek. She knew from the doctor that Chas had been sedated to help with pain relief, but continued anyway. 'I've got Cliff's Sam with me. She has been wonderful. The doctors say you are going to make a full recovery. You just need time for the cracked ribs and bruises to go down.' She smiled wanly, and then whispered so that Chas definitely couldn't hear her. 'We both need time to heal. We can go now. I know he is safe and in good hands.'

As they were leaving Sam stopped a nurse to ask whether Chas would be well enough to be questioned the following morning. She received a 'we will have to see' answer.

Sam had arranged to take Dana back to the hospital the following morning, having first ensured that Angela Chalmers would be assigned to stay with her overnight. What she hadn't told Dana was that she planned to question Chas beforehand. In her experience, it was always best to question people apart. That way you get corroborating or conflicting information. Both of which are more useful than a diluted joint statement, where people defer to one another.

As it turned out Chas proffered little more information than Dana. They both described the attackers as being of approximately the same height, definitely taller than Chas, six feet at least. And powerful. Extremely powerful. They were dressed identically, in black, both wore black Adidas trainers. 'Yes,' Dana had said, 'they had the three white stripes on the side. I know because my grandson will only wear Adidas. The others aren't cool enough apparently.'

The sole additional insight Chas could give, was that the one who spoke had a very gruff and affected voice. Almost as if he were disguising himself. When Sam pushed as to whether he could be someone Chas knew, he shook his head. 'Of course, I know people of all shapes and sizes, but two so similar who go around together like that. I've been lying here wracking my brains: bowls, golf, Daventry Conservative Club, but nobody springs to mind. Sorry.'

In the house, Angela poured Sam the final cup of tea from the pot. Dana had excused herself. She needed to 'tidy herself up'.

'How's she doing? Sam asked, taking a sip of the now lukewarm tea.

'She is amazingly strong,' replied Angela, clearly full of admiration, 'but she keeps shedding a tear, like there is something eating away at her.'

During the drive to the hospital, Sam told her of her earlier visit. 'I needed to get it done, but I didn't want to get in your way.'

'Thank you for being so considerate. It's great to hear how much he has already improved.'

'I know,' countered Sam. 'So, why is this strong and powerful person not holding onto that positive?' Sam flinched inside, wondering whether she had a right to be so forthright. With other people, such an experience could be with them for the rest of their lives. Dana didn't fit that category.

'I'm scared of telling Chas. Telling him what happened in detail. We never keep secrets, but this time I might have to. I don't want to hurt him any more than he has been already.'

'Do you think he will love you less?'

'Of course not.' There it was. That certainty borne out of the confidence in their love.

'Then tell him,' urged Sam.

Sam stopped outside the ward, which was apparently usually used by the day surgery department, and allowed Dana to go in alone. 'This is the one time I'm grateful for the doctor strikes,' she mused. For such a delicate conversation, they needed privacy. And on their own there, in that room meant for four patients, they had some.

Seeing the conversation unfold through glass, it was as if she were watching and episode of 'Casualty'. At first, she saw smiles. But then the smiling faces became more serious.

'Did he rape you?' Chas was both panicked and full of rage.

'No, he didn't. He couldn't. He used one of my candles. But, he was stopped by the other one. I suppose after you answered his questions.'

'So, he didn't really hurt you? You are telling me everything?'

'I think he was going to. I was lucky. He tried to scare me. It was stupid really.'

'What do you mean?'

'He tried to intimidate. He pushed it wick first in a bit. Then he twirled it in his left hand and pushed it a bit in butt first. I think that's…..'

Chas interrupted her. 'You mean he did it like this?' Chas performed an action he had seen only a few days before.

'Yes,' replied Dana, 'exactly like that. But he only did it the two times. How did you know what it looked like?'

'Because I know who it is. We will get the bastard.' With that he beckoned Sam to come in. He needed to tell her about Hereford.

Chapter 20

Cliff, slightly bleary eyed, emerged through the sliding doors of the baggage reclaim area. In the arrivals zone of any airport you can see a myriad of emotions: sadness from some, realising they are returning from their holiday to the stress or humdrum of day-to-day life; excitement for those being reunited; a driven purpose for some on a mission, maybe work related and, in Cliff's case as he dragged his wheeled-luggage behind him, tiredness after a sleepless long-haul flight.

His demeanour changed when he saw the smiling face of his daughter, framed by the upturned collar of her overcoat, and heard the pure joy in her voice as she shouted, 'dad, over here'.

Whilst awaiting updates on Chas and Dana, Cliff had often been distracted. He hated being so far from the action, yet in Alejo he had found a special person. For his part, Alejo had endeared himself to Cliff even more in the sensitive way he accepted Cliff's mood-swings. Knowing that his return flight was only 48 hours away, Cliff never thought about changing his flight, but, as they kept themselves occupied by doing various pieces of tourism, he would frequently check his phone for any updates. Their lovemaking became gentler and more tactile. For Cliff, this body contact was needed. Although, he could often be a little depressive, he prided himself on being a strong and resourceful person. Especially when the chips were down. However, he also knew that the love and support of others gave him more strength. When news of the assault and home invasion arrived, he excused himself by going to the bathroom. He needed to process the news on his own. He then went back to Alejo, who was patiently waiting for him on the sofa, and hugged him tightly. They stayed that way for a long time. The farewell at the airport was formal and stiff. They had said their real goodbyes back in the apartment and in the car they had held hands, or lovingly touched each other's thigh. Their relationship had been cemented, with Alejo planning to come over to the UK at Easter. Now Cliff had to focus on helping Chas and Dana. And finally solve the riddle that was Paddy Cullen.

As they walked through the short-stay car park, Sam updated Cliff on Chas' progress.

'The doctors are really pleased with him. They made a right mess of his face, and he still looks like a dog's dinner, but, apart from his broken ribs, he is doing well. They might even be releasing him today.'

Cliff looked like a weight had been lifted off his shoulders. 'So, no long-term damage at all?'

'No, I called Dana on the way to the airport. She says the ribs need time to heal, just like his face. Otherwise, he will be as right as rain.'

'I suppose it will be a lot of doing nothing. That will bore the hell out of him,' commented Cliff.

'Yes, Dana is panicking already. She loves him to bits, but a bored Chas, is a grumpy Chas,' replied Sam. 'Apparently, he can't lift things for a while, or do exercise, but he shouldn't stay in one position for too long either. Poor thing.'

'Flipping Heck!' Cliff was starting to laugh. 'Murray must be doing his nut. What with Paddy dead and Chas injured, that leaves only four of us in the team. Good job we had no game last week, and the leagues are shutting down for the Christmas break.'

Sam smiled, happy to see her father laughing. 'That's it, Dad. Get your priorities right.'

Cliff changed the topic. 'At least Roy is getting back later today too. I received a text saying Sinead's funeral had been quiet, but still stressful nonetheless. He was glad for Michael and Seamus' support once more.'

'They do sound a lovely family,' said Sam, pressing the button to unlock her car.

Once in the vehicle, Cliff allowed Sam to concentrate on her driving as she navigated her way out of the airport. It was one of his pet peeves, how convoluted and badly signed the route to the exit was. She had literally only just pulled onto the dual carriageway when he asked. 'What about these SAS psychos, any luck there?'

'More than you would think,' she replied, glancing quickly at Cliff. 'So much more.'

....

Based on her interview with Chas in the hospital, she had immediately driven to Paddy's house. As Chas had told them his address, it seemed logical that they would have gone there. The front of the house looked normal, but the conservatory door had been forced in no subtle way. Inside, it looked like a whirlwind had been through. It would have been easier to say what hadn't been moved, thrown or strewn, rather than what had. One thing did stand out though. The bowls cabinet had been smashed open, and, judging by a comparison with photos taken after Paddy's body had been discovered, some of its contents had been taken. The Scene of crime officers had, on Sam's request, returned to the bungalow, but found nothing which could be of forensic help.

It was only after the conversation between Chas and Dana that Sam had something definite to act upon. By identifying Mark 'Pitbull' Bull as the probable assailant who had taken Dana upstairs and assaulted her, it meant that the one who had tortured Chas was equally likely to be Tony 'Sketch' Etches. Her telephone call to the Black Boy in Credenhill gave her an address for Etches. One that she soon found out, didn't exist. As well as giving her the name of the pub he had met them in, Chas had recalled them mentioning that they had set up a personal security firm after leaving the Army. A quick search of Companies House located the rather unimaginatively named 'Etches & Bull, Private Security and Personal Safety'. This provided Sam with a landline number for the company, along with an address.

This turned out to be another example of their use of smoke and mirrors. The lady who answered the phone, purporting to be their secretary, soon caved when she realised she was speaking to a police officer.

Wrong Bias

CP Wolf

Angela Grayson, the so-called secretary, ran her own company, 'Professional Front'. Her company's role was to provide gravitas and acceptability for smaller firms which couldn't afford the necessary outlay to make it competitive in the real world. This meant that she answered a specific landline number for any given firm. Every time someone called looking to employ one of the companies, in this case 'Etches and Bull', she would either forward the call to their mobile or take a message saying they were busy in a meeting. The address on record at Companies House was also the address of 'Professional Front', so she could handle any correspondence for them. The two things anyone looking to employ a company wants were therefore provided: a landline and an address to show the company was solid and not itinerant.

From her conversation with Angela, Sam learnt that Etches and Bull hadn't been heard from in over a week. So, at that point, it looked like another dead end. That was until Angela volunteered another piece of information. Some customers also used her, for an extra charge, to take payments for them. Etches and Bull was one of the companies that did so. This meant that when Sam put the phone down on her call to Angela, she had both the account number and sort code of the company bank account.

'Blimey,' said Cliff. 'You found all that out so quickly. That's amazing.'

'Unfortunately,' replied Sam. 'That's where everything slowed for a few hours as I had to pass it on. It's not like on TV. You can't just type in a bank account number. People have rights and banks protect the privacy of their customers.'

'I suppose so.' Cliff sounded a bit flat. 'So, what did you do? What could you do?'

'I went right to the top,' she replied.

'What, God?' Cliff laughed, knowing now there was going to be a positive outcome.

'No, the Masons.' Sam and Cliff laughed together as one. They had always done so before he left her mother, Julia, and they were back in the habit of doing it again. It just felt right, laughing together even at the merest of things. 'DI Bridges, of course. I went to him. It's a big case. He knew it was the only lead we had. And a good one.'

'I suppose he made a few calls, or did some funky handshakes,' said Cliff.

'Something like that. I don't really know. I guess it's like dominoes. He knows someone from the lodge in banking, maybe a different bank. And then they know someone else, nearer the target. Eventually the domino must have fallen at the feet of the right person, because, an hour later, Bridges plonked a printout of their bank account on my desk.'

'Wow! I can only imagine what Roy would say to this. He would be blowing a gasket about how this country is run by people lurking in the shadows.' Cliff chuckled, imagining steam coming out of his friend's ears.

'Well, in this case, I was grateful for the old boy network. It got us no closer to catching them, but it gave us an insight into why they might be so desperate.'

'How so?' Cliff asked

'They were so much in debt, Dad. The overdraft was at its limit and they had just had a substantial consolidation loan turned down.'

'And desperate men do desperate things,' sighed Cliff, trying not to picture the savagery of the home invasion.

'Yes,' replied Sam, 'but they didn't kill Paddy. We guessed that from Chas' conversation with them in the Black Boy. Now we have checked their alibi, too.'

'Alibi? What alibi?' Cliff looked stunned. 'How can you know what their alibi is?' He paused, before adding. 'You've found them. Haven't you?'

Sam had been smirking, enjoying watching her father trying to piece things together. He used to tease her about what she was getting for Christmas and Birthdays. Now it was her turn. She knew the word 'alibi' would have got his brain cells going.

'Well, we had already put out an APW, of course.' She was just going to taunt Cliff a little bit more.

'APW? Stop it Sam.' Cliff was all but raising his voice. 'Just tell me.' His tone just had that hint of desperation that caused Sam to melt.

'All ports warning,' she clarified. 'We were struggling to locate them. We certainly didn't want them skulking off out of our jurisdiction.'

'Very clever,' said Cliff calming down a bit. 'That worked then?'

'It did. Surprisingly so.'

With their passport details obtained and circulated, more as a matter of procedure than expectation, Sam had been briefing DI Bridges when she received a call from a Border Force Sergeant working at Heathrow. Bull and Etches had been identified when they were checking in their luggage for a flight to Buenos Aries. The Border Force officers then played the two men as if they were fish already caught on the line, allowing them to proceed, as normal, through to departures. With their luggage already having been siphoned off from the rest of the passengers on that flight, armed officers quickly and without fuss arrested them as they were clearing security. That way, the officers could be certain that Etches and Bull weren't carrying anything which could be used as weapons. Also, by asking the second of them in the queue, Bull, to go to the special screening scanner, it separated the two dangerous men even more.

'Very clever,' commented Cliff. 'Would have thought it would have been difficult to get them to talk though. After all, they are trained to withstand virtually anything.'

'Oh ye of little faith. To doubt your daughter so.'

'You did the interview? I thought they were at Heathrow.'

'Well, I did have to come here anyway, the following day, to pick up some grumpy old sod. So, I suggested to the Border Force guys that they keep them there for me. In separate rooms, of course, while I packed a bag and got my evidence sorted out. I knew their facilities were much more modern than what we have at our little regional station. Shelley Wilde, my DS, came along too. Two suspects, two interviewers. She went home last night, though. Her husband is on shift work, and she couldn't get a babysitter at such short notice.'

As Cliff had suspected, Bull and Etches weren't going to admit to anything. Rather cockily, they denied legal representation, and just sat there, almost side on to the interviewers saying, 'no comment' to every question. Although Sam and Shelley had arrived in separate cars, they had used the journey time to formulate, via phone, their plan of attack.

They knew it best not to play all their cards at once. So, after stating why they were there, they slowly piled on the evidence against the guys: the fact they had recently met and spoken to one of the victims; CCTV evidence from the Maple leaf garage in Daventry, clearly identifying them as being in the area on the night of the attack; the same footage showing them as wearing the clothing described by the victims, right down to the adidas trainers they were still wearing in the interview rooms at Heathrow airport.

At this point, they still hadn't broken them. Bull had shifted in his seat, when the trainers were mentioned, but Etches had remained totally passive throughout the whole process. Sam and Shelley, then focussed on the sexual assault. They said that convicted sex offenders, no matter how hard and tough they were, always had to be on the lookout when in prison. Those sort of offenders were identified as fair game, and usually had to beg to be kept apart from the main population. Normally, with the other 'nonces' and 'sickos'. 'Imagine that,' they said, 'spending all day, every day with rapists and paedos'. Bull, having heard this, looked down at the ground, but Etches gave a more visible response. He looked angry.

The coup de grâce came when they mentioned the twirling trick with the left-hand. At this point, Etches asked for a lawyer. He wasn't going to be locked away with perverts because Bull went too far.

Fortunately for Sam and Shelley, a duty solicitor is on permanent call at the airport. Normally, the requests are from someone who is seeking asylum or has been caught smuggling drugs. After a brief consultation with his legal advisor, Etches said that he was prepared to tell them everything on two conditions: firstly, that the judge of any prosecution be made aware of his cooperation with the police and secondly, any charges he faced would not refer to the sexual assault. Shelley, sensing this might be the case, had already phoned DI Bridges and then the CPS, Crown Prosecution Service, to see what they could offer the first one to ask for a deal – more than likely the one who didn't take Dana upstairs. Knowing that Etches was still likely to get the maximum of five years imprisonment for what was a serious example of ABH (Actual Bodily Harm), and that it would be hard to prove that Etches sanctioned the sexual element of the assault, the CPS gave the go ahead for him not to be charged with sexual assault. Given that he was the main aggressor, any judge would not be swayed by his belated cooperation. He was, after all, a trained killer, using the skills given to him by his country to cause one of its citizens great suffering.

Etches told Sam and Shelley of the surprise they had felt when hearing that Paisley, under the assumed name of Paddy Cullen, had just recently been killed. They thought he had died many years before. When Paisley rejoined his regiment from his undercover work in Derry, he did so having gained the knowledge that Argentinian gold was coming over from Tierra del Fuego to help fund the terrorist activities of the IRA. This knowledge he shared with his two best mates, Bull and Etches. They still had a few more years to serve before they could leave the service. So, knowing the situation in Ireland was going to run and run, they used the time wisely to research the area and the military base there. When the Argentinian forces invaded the Falklands, they couldn't believe their luck. They knew their squadron, Z squadron, above any other would be sent there. If nothing more it would allow them to study the area first hand, but as it turned out Z squadron was selected for a reconnaissance mission on the island itself. Six soldiers were to spend one week there, spying on the base, reporting back on any activity they saw. Paisley, Etches and Bull made sure they got selected. They didn't expect to find the gold store, but could at least get some potential locations for them to come back to after the war.

On the fourth night there, they saw a lorry drive through the main gates. What piqued their interest was that it wasn't a military lorry, but a commercial one. They observed as it went to what looked like a missile silo. The two drivers already had keys to the padlocks which they opened and were then seen descending some steps. A few minutes later they returned carrying one large solitary box. On its side was printed, 'vajilla y cubertería'. They put it in the back of the lorry, having put the padlocks back on, and exited through the main gates. Not being Spanish speakers, the soldiers pulled out the dictionary they had been supplied with. 'Crockery and cutlery,' Paisley had laughed. 'That's it. That's where the fucking gold is.'

The next night there was a lot of low cloud. So, under the cover of darkness, they returned and, because of the lax security, they literally just walked in and were able to steal as much gold as they could carry. A hiding spot, a few kilometres away, had already been chosen for the gold. The plan was to return once the one-sided war had been won, and to smuggle the bullion back to the UK, or maybe to somewhere in Europe.

Sam interrupted Etches at this point and asked. 'How were you going to do this?'

'We used to drink with a pilot assigned to the regiment,' replied Etches. 'His name was Wyn 'Taffy' Evans. He was a good guy, but, one day he just resigned his commission. You see he had close relatives in Argentina, who had told him the war was likely. And he wasn't going to fight them. So, before it really kicked off, he decided to jump ship and go to join them. It was nowhere near any potential war zone, and they had been nagging him to go there for years.'

'The three of you were planning to use him to fly the gold to another part of Argentina,' Shelley said.

'Yes, in Patagonia somewhere. We didn't know exactly. He was more Paisley's mate. They were the ones who kept in touch. So, when we thought Paisley had died, our plan died too. We just couldn't work out how to get the gold out. We almost went mad, knowing it was there for the collecting.'

'How were you going to ship it out?' Shelley persisted.

'Where there are cows, there are cowboys and horses. And horses need horseshoes and blacksmiths. That's what Taffy's family does out there. We were going to smelt the gold and convert them to sport's trophies.'

Sam realised that Paisley had been the brains behind the operation, and he had kept vital facts from these two. He probably even withheld the exact GPS coordinates of where the bullion was stashed. She had never seen images of the area, but reckoned it was similar to Snowdonia or Dartmoor, isolated and bleak. It'd be nigh on impossible to find a specific spot without any navigation aid. That explained the real reason they hadn't gone to retrieve the gold themselves. She could have pointed this out and belittled him, but he was singing like a bird and she didn't want to stop him.

'Why now?' This was the tack she chose. 'Why look for the gold now?'

Etches shifted in his chair. 'Look at us,' he finally said. 'We ain't getting any younger. Personal security is active work and recently we've struggled to pay ourselves any wages at all, let alone employ others. That's why we were there, in Hereford. Hate those bloody reunions, but we were desperate. Hoped, as former comrades in arms, we might get some work out of going there.'

'And did you?'

'Did we fuck! Half of them were so up their own arses about being former captain of the golf club, and the like. They weren't interested in talking to us. Some wouldn't even give us the time of day after we mentioned our line of work. Then those two blow us away with the fact Paisley had only just died. That got us remembering, thinking about the gold, like. Just maybe we had a way out.'

'What was your plan?'

'We didn't have one. We just followed their car. When matey, the one with the prissy hair, got to what must have been his house, we just sat outside working out what to do. We needed to know everything he did. And, more importantly, we needed to hunt down 'Taffy' Evans.'

'And did you?' Shelley asked.'

'Too bloody easily, actually,' he replied, with more than a hint of frustration. 'Should have thought of it before. We've both got small army pensions and realised Evans was old enough to draw one himself. Entitled too. Bull's most recent ex works for Veterans UK and they administer the service pensions. Bull threw her a line about wanting to contact an old comrade and luckily she saw no harm in looking into it for us. Turns out he lives in some town called

Gaiman. On the map it looks like it's in the back of beyond.'

'Knowing where you might find Evans, made getting the information from Chas Findus even more relevant,' concluded Sam.

'Findus, is that his name?' Etches replied. 'Yes, we were certainly more driven by getting the lead on Evans. In a way he should be thanking me for being the one to have worked him over. Old Bull just doesn't know when to stop. Stupid sod was only supposed to scare her, or maybe slap her a bit. Something her husband could hear downstairs.'

'But you did imply that Bull might be going to molest her up there,' interjected Shelley.

'That was just to get him talking. I certainly didn't think Bull was doing what he did.' He paused, looking first at Sam and then at Shelley. 'Besides, as soon as I knew he'd told me everything he could, I called on Bull to leave.'

'Very noble, I'm sure.' Shelley couldn't hide her sarcasm, as she thought of what poor Dana had been through. 'You went from there straight to Paisley's house?'

'Yes, it was still dark, so it made sense. We really wanted to find some details of the bank account. To get us access you see.' Sam nodded. 'But we couldn't find sweet FA about the bank.'

'You did take some things though,' said Sam. 'From the cabinet.'

'Yes, we left with two gold bowls trophies. We used a knife to scrape the outer layer of paint off. We did it to all of them, but only two were gold. That was our gold. And it made us want more.'

'Technically not your gold,' thought Sam. What she did say was. 'What then?'

'We knew the heat might be on, so we took them to a guy I know. He runs a pawn shop, and I know he fences stolen goods from time to time. He gave us a fair price. Going to Argentina seemed a logical step. Out of the reach of the law, and maybe getting hold of more gold through Evans.'

……………..

'That brings you up to speed,' said Sam, turning into the drive of Cliff's house. 'Shelley went home, I ate and slept in the Premier Inn at the airport, preferring that to driving back again in the morning to get you. And Bull and Etches are being transferred this afternoon to our nick. Not sure when they are having their remand hearings.' She turned the ignition off. 'What are your plans?'

'Going to grab a few hours sleep. Roy should be back later. If Chas is up to it, we will catch up first thing in the morning. I might phone Alejo too,' he added, with a twinkle in his eye. 'He might earn some brownie points if I pass on what we now know about the gold and Evans in Gaiman. Thanks luv, you really are some policewoman.' He pecked her on the cheek and got out of the car. She was just about to reverse out of the drive when her father turned around and started to wave his arms, gesturing for her to wind down the window.

'What about their alibi for Paddy?' Cliff asked, leaning in through the driver's window. 'You never got around to telling me that.'

'Oops!' Sam was smiling. 'I should have started with that, shouldn't I. When we were getting their passport details, we noticed they weren't in the country that weekend. I suppose for the police it's one advantage of Brexit. What with people needing immigration stamps to get in and out of Europe now.'

'Where were they then? Thought they hadn't much work.'

'Spain,' she replied, 'According to Etches, they were acting as personal security guards for a cocker spaniel who was favourite to win best in breed at the Seville equivalent of Crufts.'

'Well that alibi really takes the biscuit.' Cliff was shaking with laughter. 'Well a Bonio, anyway.'

Chapter 21

Cliff waited until they were on their own back in his car until he shared his concerns with Roy.

'What do you think?'

'About what?' Roy replied. His mind was already back on the date he'd organised with Judith.

'Don't you think something wasn't quite right?'

'Well, I did think it strange we weren't offered biscuits or cake, but put it down to what they'd been through.'

'I give up.' Cliff should have known that Roy was about as perceptive as a plank of wood. Sam had been professional in not sharing all the details of the sexual assault on Dana with her father, and Cliff had shared even less with Roy. 'I think we need to keep an eye on both of them. I can't begin to appreciate what they went through with those bastards. They are putting on a brave front, but there were looks between them that really worried me.'

Roy could have kicked himself for his insensitivity. 'You are right. I suppose I just wanted them to be on the mend, and was only looking for the positives.'

'The good news is that he is housebound for the time being, and Dana isn't going to leave him alone. That means together they can take the time they need to mend.'

'Is that why you divided the tasks as you did?'

....

Initially, the focus had been on the home invasion and Dana and Chas' health, but the couple soon turned the conversation back to the investigation. They said that there was no point in looking back, particularly as the assailants had been arrested and charged. It would never have happened, had they not been investigating the death of Paddy Cullen. It would be for nought if the murderer were never found.

With cups of tea being poured, they went over everything they now knew. The Argentinian investigation seemed to have come to a conclusion, with that having no clear connection to the murder. On the other hand, the Irish link still might provide the answer. The attempts on Roy were linked to Paisley. And with the two who probably carried out both attacks also being associated to the family where he lodged, this suggested the killing may have been related to his time in Derry. Roy, because of his sources and friends there, was given the task to pursue that further. But preferably without putting his life at risk by going back there. What exactly he could do, apart from liaising with Declan, to further that side of the investigation, nobody really knew.

Chas suggested they look at other pathways, ones they had initially discarded. The first was to go back to the car SatNav data. As well as going to the airports, he had gone to various bowls clubs. Cliff volunteered to do the rounds. As a member of the club's county league team, he too had played at most of the same rinks as Paddy. Therefore, the people at these clubs knew him and might talk to him.

That left Paddy's trips to Spain. They had assumed these were simple bowling holidays in the sun. Chas and Dana were going to use modern technology and follow that tenuous lead from home.

....

Cliff put the car into drive and set off for his house.

'Do you think we are closing in on the killer, or is our chance of success getting smaller?' Roy asked his friend this, as he texted Judith.

'Not sure mate,' replied Cliff, slightly shocked by the depth of the question. Or maybe more shocked by its source. 'Hope it's the former. We need a bit of luck.'

Chapter 22

Roy sat at the small dining room table, staring without purpose at the blank screen of his iPad. His mind should have been on the imminent incoming call, but he was distracted. Distracted, by thoughts of romance and sex. Distracted, as each of his senses, one by one, imagined the overload they would experience. Distracted by thoughts of the fair Judith.

His day hadn't started out with any lofty expectation. In fact, he had been primed for disappointment. With the golf course open once more, that meant the 'old farts' were back in action. At Staverton Park, you have the Men's Section, no further explanation needed, then you have the

Seniors' Section, for over 55-year-olds who play in the week as well as at the weekend. The further to the edge you go, age wise, means you gravitate to your own particular 'old fart' group. Like minded men, who need more than the Seniors' Section can provide. Roy was a long-term member of such a group, and Chas had recently joined it as well. Cliff, being a bit younger, wasn't quite in that category, preferring to play less regularly with his weekend four ball. Mack Merlin and Percy Johns, like Cliff were in the Seniors' Section. Only Clive Wilton, an ex-prison warden, kept his distance totally. 'I'm not playing with the Walking Dead.' A bit of a golfing snob, if truth be told.

On every day when there is no official competition, they will play nine holes in groups of three or four and then assemble in the bar area for pots of tea or coffee, consumed with whatever free biscuit the bar manager may have chosen to offset the ridiculously high beverage costs. As well as discussing their various ailments, they will pretend they are twenty years younger, and physically more potent, by flirting with the friendly bar staff. If it is someone's birthday, or something special needs to be celebrated, then they are permitted to bring in some extra appropriate nibbles.

With Christmas approaching, they had got into the habit of providing, in turns, some such treat.

Normally, given the stingy nature of the group it was something going stale that 'the wife baked yesterday' or a sale item from Lidl or Aldi. Going there that morning Roy knew that it was the turn of Grayston McPartick, him of the infamous 'Burn's night leftover wraps'. There had been a vote on their WhatsApp group whether to ban him, but he had fierce loyal support from Tom Connolly and Phil Frienden, who got his punishment commuted to a written warning. This warning must have done its job, because Grayston turned up with five boxes of 'Waitrose extra buttery luxury and scrumptious deeply filled mince pies'. And very nice they were too.

As there were too many for the group, Roy had smuggled a few of the uneaten pies out, without the normally eagle-eyed Grayston noticing. He had remembered Judith saying how she was a 'sucker' for a good mince pie. 'Maybe that might not happen until the second date,' mused Roy, as he drove the short distance to the bowls club. 'I can wait. For a bit anyway.' Judith had seemed so pleased to see him when he walked into the bowls club that he reckoned she would have agreed to the date anyway. Maybe there was no need for the tasty bribe, but then he would have missed her tongue sweeping up the buttery crumbs from around her lips. 'It's like my own personal flake advert,' he thought.

Roy's daydreaming came to an abrupt halt when the familiar whistling WhatsApp ringtone, set annoyingly on full volume, broke the silence. The forefinger of his right hand automatically pressed the green button, and the now familiar faces of Michael Kelly and Declan O'Shaughnessy filled the screen. Roy smiled, as his new best friend shifted in his seat, wetting down the little that was left of his hair at the same time. It was Michael who spoke first. 'Great to see you Roy. You're looking well. Declan contacted me this morning saying he had something to tell us both. As you had scheduled this call, I thought it made sense for him to join us. Hope you don't mind?'

'Mind? Of course not, Michael,' replied Roy. 'We were only looking for a catch up. We've hit a bit of a dead end and thought it worth looking back at the Derry connection.' He went on to fill them in on recent events and new developments in their investigation. He did this out of courtesy to the other two, knowing that Declan wouldn't be there had he not got something significant to share. 'So, you can see we are having to re-examine lines of enquiry, such as Derry, or go into more detail on ones we felt less important like his SatNav data,' he concluded. 'Declan, something tells me you aren't here for a chin wag. Say I'm not wrong.'

'You most certainly aren't wrong, Roy,' answered the police officer. 'Things have really developed over here. Things that might mean you and your friends aren't safe over there in England.'

After the abortive attempt on Roy's life in Derry the week before, there had been a massive manhunt for Micky O'Donovan and Thomas Ahern. It had been an island-wide endeavour with full media support and coverage. 'An Garda Siochána', the police force of the Irish Republic, because of the open borders and therefore easy freedom of movement, had also been put on high alert. Despite their photos being on every news bulletin and across the front pages of every daily newspaper, there was no sniff of these two dangerous men. The hotlines in Derry police station, manned 24/7, were silent. Not even a hoax call had come in.

Then out of the blue, they received a creditable tip. A life-long criminal, on remand for serious Class A drug offences, saw his chance to negotiate a deal for a reduced sentence. When the deal was signed, and in the pocket of his solicitor, he gave the police an address in the Short Strand, a working-class inner city Catholic area of Belfast.

The police set up a perimeter to ensure there would be no escape, and then as soon as darkness fell, a full squad of armed police were sent in.

Unfortunately, Ahern and O'Donovan were alerted by a screaming baby, unhappy at having been woken up. Collateral damage is something to be avoided and the houses either side of the address they had been given, needed to be cleared by the police before the front door of the hideaway could be breached. With the element of surprise having been taken away, a gunfight ensued. Three police officers were killed and another five were currently recovering in hospital as a result. Thomas Ahern was also among the deceased. He had been at the top of the stairs using his semi automatic rifle to take out anyone who entered through the front door. It was only when his gun jammed that he was overpowered, and in trying to wrestle a firearm from a police officer, he was mortally wounded as that weapon discharged two rounds.

'What about O'Donovan?' Roy asked, having listened intently without interrupting. If their lives were still in danger, then he already knew the answer. He just hoped he was wrong.

'He got away,' said Declan, with a sigh. 'He must have slipped out the back quite early on in the fight.'

'I thought you had the area surrounded,' interjected Michael.

'We did, but we reckon he jumped into the river behind the house, and swam across it.'

'That's the Lagan isn't it?' Michael looked amazed. Declan nodded. 'But that's at least fifty metres wide. He must be some swimmer.'

'I get that he got away, but why do you think we are in danger over here?'

'Because Ahern had both a passport and a driving licence on him,' replied Declan. 'Fake ones, but impossible to tell from the real thing. He had changed his appearance somewhat to match the photo in it. No wonder we got no calls on the tip line. O'Donovan will have done the same. Those documents will allow him to move about as he wants.'

'But he could go anywhere. Couldn't he?'

'Maybe, but he's tried twice to get you in Derry, and that was weeks apart.' Declan paused, before continuing. 'I wouldn't bet against him wanting to finish the job off. We know there's a personal link to all of this.'

'What about his scar over the eye? That'll stand out when he's going through passport control.' Roy realised he was clutching at straws.

'You'd be amazed how things like that get missed. Chances are he's on the mainland already.' Declan's matter of fact delivery, made Roy's heart miss a beat.

'Thanks guys. I'd better let Cliff and Chas know. God knows how Chas will feel when he hears the news. He has been through enough'. He thanked Michael and Declan and signed off, having promised Michael he would text him every day.

....

'So you'll contact Chas?' Roy had just updated Cliff.
'I suppose so,' replied Cliff. 'Why can't you do it? I'm driving.'
'Because I've got to get the annex cleaned for Judith. She's coming over this evening.'
'A date! Bloody hell, Roy. Talk about getting your priorities right.'
'Believe me, I have. If there is a scarf tied around the handle of the front door, please stay away.'
'You've been watching too many corny films.' With that Cliff hung up.

Chapter 23

Cliff had decided to pull over. He needed to absorb the implications of Roy's rather disturbing phone call. Unlike his lodger, he wasn't going to be so gung-ho in his attitude, and would be extra vigilant. He had already made sure that no car immediately behind him had pulled into the same lay-by. Although Roy had been the target in Derry, that did not mean that any of the rest of them, including Bertie, were not necessarily at risk.

Using the seamlessly smooth Bluetooth system on his Lexus, he found Chas' home number in the directory, and called him. Dana answered the phone on the second ring. Her hushed tones told Cliff that Chas was nearby, and probably resting. Time wasn't on his side, he had a lot still to do that day, so as succinctly as possible he outlined the threat to Dana. He could have been more reassuring in his tone, but that would have defeated the object of the call; to warn the rest of the team about O'Donovan.

After ending the call with Dana, he then contacted Sam. He knew the police might not be able to react to such a flimsy threat, but his daughter would. As hoped, and already semi-promised to Dana in the previous call, Sam said she would cash in a few favours with the uniform officers, by asking them to be as visible as possible around the houses of Cliff and Chas. He had earlier audibly sighed with relief when Dana had informed him of Bertie's whereabouts; on an all-inclusive cruise just off Antigua.

'Lucky bugger,' Cliff had thought. 'Think we might all need to go on one of those when this is all over.'

Cliff reached over to the passenger's seat to pick up the AA road map of the UK, which was already open on the relevant double page. Although he habitually used the car's SatNav or Apple CarPlay, he had prior to his departure sat down with the road map and, together with the printout from Paddy's destinations, used a blue marker pen to trace out the most efficient route to cover as many of the bowls clubs as quickly as possible. He knew he had a maximum of three days to get to all of the clubs before they shut down for the Christmas holidays.

Equipped with multiple copies of pictures depicting Paisley, the young soldier, and Paisley, as the older Paddy, Roy had spent the morning visiting clubs to the south and west. The rinks had been full at Bicester, Oxford and Aylesbury Vale, but nobody really helped further the investigation. Most people had never seen him, and those that had, commented on him as a bowler only; a great competitor, who was a brilliant ambassador for Daventry Indoor Bowling Club. He asked permission to put one of each of the pictures up on the notice board, along with a flyer asking for any information or recollections people might have about the person. At the bottom of the flyer was his name and mobile number.

He started to enter the next few destinations into the system, firstly Northampton and then Kingsthorpe. He liked the former, both as a location and as a rink. Kingsthorpe, on the other hand, had a beautiful bowling surface, but the parking there was far from adequate. That negative thought made Cliff pause for a while, his eyes following the whole route, which was divided into two loops. One for each of the days he expected to be travelling, with each loop ending back in Daventry.

He started to feel a little edgy. There was something he was missing. The more he sat there thinking, trying to make sense of this feeling, the more agitated he became. To Cliff, there had never been anything more frustrating than to have something on the tip of your tongue, or to have an unexplained anxiety, without being able to identify it.

He knew it wouldn't come to him, so he shut his eyes and took his mind back through what had happened: finding Paddy's body, searching his home for clues; the investigation going off to all parts of the UK and even to South America; Alejo, a new wonderful lover; the smuggled gold to Northern Ireland; the home invasion of Chas and Dana; Etches' confession.

His eyes opened with a start. 'That's' it!' He looked at the right-hand page of the map, and then down at the SatNav print from Paddy's car. It wasn't there. Desborough wasn't on the list. Why not? Paddy used to boast about how well he bowled there. He won their open two years running. There was a framed picture next to the trophy cabinet from the Northamptonshire Telegraph with Paddy holding the Desborough Cup aloft. Yet, in the last two years, or since he had acquired his new car, he hadn't bowled there. Sometimes people carpool to away venues. Not Paddy. He needed 'to focus on the task ahead'. To

Cliff, there was no logical reason for Paddy not to include Desborough in his schedule.

'Maybe I won't need to go to bloody Kingsthorpe after all,' he thought, as he entered a new postcode into the system.

Chapter 24

Dana decided to let Chas sleep, despite the ominous nature of Cliff's call. In her mind, rest was what Chas needed, and thirty minutes here or there wouldn't make a blind bit of difference. Chas, of course, saw things differently. No sooner had Dana explained things to him than he was up like a shot, running around securing all external doors and making sure the little keys on the triple-glazed windows were properly locked.

'We should have done this after the attack,' he said, after he had phoned 'Easisafe Home Security' to purchase their platinum package. 'It's a bit like being in the ICU at hospital, rather than in a large general ward. We will be put into our own small elite group of houses, which is constantly monitored through

CCTV by dedicated 'Easisafe Guardians'. That means real people protecting us. Whereas, if you purchase the bronze package, you rely on the technology alone. They will install ultra-High definition, state of the art, cameras ensuring there is not a blind spot anywhere, and....'

'How much does it cost?' Dana interrupted. 'Last month, you cancelled my Spotify account, because 'it's not cost effective'. Dana wasn't one to harbour grudges, but she missed listening to whatever she wanted whenever the mood so took her. Now she had to put up with bloody Alexa's generic choice.

'You can't put a price on our safety, luv.'

'I know, but just because we fancy steak, it doesn't mean we need to buy fillet. You know you will regret it, when you see the monthly statements. Besides, Cliff's getting Sam to organise us some more police presence in the road.'

Chas looked deflated. 'Can't we at least get the bronze package? Better locks on the windows and five 4K cameras hooked up to their centralised automated detection system.' Chas looked with puppy dog eyes at his wife, before adding. 'Please?' Dana caved. Whenever Chas resorted to elongated, single word or short phrase pleading, she could do nothing but give in to his demands.

'Make sure the contract is no longer than an initial twelve months.'

'Ok,' replied a relieved Chas, as he picked up the house phone again. 'We have a fourteen day call off period so we can do that, no quibbles. Although we will be paying them a lot less money, at least we aren't cancelling altogether. So they won't be too upset with us.'

Dana nodded and went off to make a pot of tea. 'When I come back it will be time to talk to Benidorm.'

When Chas and Dana had been assigned the job of researching Paddy's trip to Benidorm, Chas thought of Roger Hellman from the bowls club. The Hellmans were stalwart supporters of the club; all nine of them. Roy often joked that if you were never more than ten yards from a rat, then at the bowls club, there was always a Hellman even closer.

Roger Hellman often bowled in a shirt he purchased from a club in Menorca. Cliff and he had once been opposing skips in a triples match, which meant they spent two hours, alone, at the other end to the bowlers. Time enough, in fact to discuss many things. The topic of bowling in Spain had indeed come up, and Chas was certain that Benidorm was one place where Roger had played. So, before his lunchtime nap, Chas had contacted him at home.

Roger, it turned out, used to go there regularly many years ago, probably before Paddy's trips, as he had no recollection of seeing him there. What he could provide though was a contact number for the ex-pat who was President of the Finca Guila Bowls Club

'Can I speak to Julian Poulter? My name is Chas Findus,' Chas asked, when he heard a female voice answer the phone. He had the phone on speakerphone so that Dana would be able to hear everything.

'I am sorry, he has been held up at a meeting in town. He should be home soon. Maybe I can be of help? I'm his wife.' Her clipped home-counties voice conveyed total confidence, probably from being used to having to stand in for her husband.

'Well, I don't see why not. We were friends of Paddy Cullen.'

'Were?' The interruption was spontaneous and spiked with emotion. The follow up though was more controlled. 'Are you saying he is dead?'

'I'm afraid so,' replied Chas. 'He was murdered in his home last month. We are helping his solicitor try to locate potential heirs.'

'I'm sorry to hear that.' Her voice sounded almost forced. 'We knew Paddy quite well. He came here to bowl, and get away from the cold weather back home of course. As for family, we only ever saw him on his own.'

Dana broke the short silence. 'Hello, I'm Chas's wife. Paddy's death has opened a real can of worms. He was not who we thought he was. And, if I'm guessing correctly, not the man you thought you knew.' She paused. 'And had feelings for.'

Chas looked shocked. 'What?' he mouthed.

'How did you know?' The voice at the other end of the phone had given up trying to hide any emotion. What had previously been clipped and controlled, was now breathy and higher pitched.

By the time Alison Poulter's husband finally arrived home, and the call was slightly prematurely ended, Chas and Dana knew the full story. Paddy had met the very bored and sexually frustrated Alison on one of his many Iberian bowling breaks. They had been playing as leads on opposite teams one morning, and that's when they had bonded. Paddy had been his usual witty and entertaining self, and Alison, once more deserted by her financier husband who had gone to Frankfurt, saw a chance to bring some fun into her life. Dinner begat sex, which in turn begat love. Paddy returned as often as possible, usually timing it to coincide with Julian's business trips away. Unfortunately, one evening they became complacent and were seen, by another equally bored and jealous housewife, holding hands on the promenade. That woman got drunk and told her husband, informing him that she envied Alison. He, in turn, gleefully told Julian, and anyone else he could. Julian had black-balled him from being vice-captain of the club, and this was his revenge. Julian, a perennial bully, immediately confronted Paddy, not knowing of his SAS background, and ended up in hospital with a broken arm and multiple cuts and bruising. Paddy disappeared that day and never returned. Alison would have willingly gone with him, but, as he had told her multiple times, he wasn't a person made for a life-time commitment.

That had all blown up in February. Since then, Alison and Julian had tried to rekindle some semblance of a happy marriage. They may have fooled many, but their closer friends knew things hadn't really changed. Julian was once again leaving Alison alone as he started to increase the number of business trips, and although Alison had been throwing herself into supporting more and more charities, such as the local donkey sanctuary, she was hardly ever seen smiling.

Dana, whose gentle non-judgmental empathy had put Alison at ease, had been on the point of discussing her financial situation should they divorce, when Julian arrived home and Alison abruptly had to finish the call.

'Poor thing,' Dana said, as she put the phone back in its cradle. 'I'm going to call her again tomorrow.'

Chas looked at his wife in admiration. No matter the situation, Dana always could find the time to help others.

'Yes, think she'd appreciate that. We do know one thing.'

'What's that?'

'Well unless Julian grew a pair, and was in the UK at the time, I can't see Paddy's trip to Spain having anything to do with the murder.'

'When I call tomorrow, I will check on his whereabouts, and whether he might have sought revenge.'

Chas collected their mugs, and went out to make another cup of tea. They may not have conclusively excluded Benidorm from the investigation, but his gut told him otherwise.

Chapter 25

Desborough is secreted in the eastern side of Northamptonshire, a few minutes northwest of Kettering. Although it may not be the most pleasant of journeys for any travelling Daventry bowler, the facility itself more than makes up for any traffic jams you may encounter on the A14. The green carpet of the six-rink club was famous countywide for its fast true running nature, and the coffee machine, unlike the one Cliff and the others had to turn to when Judith's café was shut, was actually fully functioning, accepting both card and coin. Using the one in Daventry, when it wasn't broken nor empty of ingredients, was like taking a Mensa exam.

    Cliff was happy that the rerouting of his pre-planned investigation loop avoided the A14, allowing him instead to arrive from the south on the A43. During the journey, he had been pondering his decision to abandon his plans, and go directly there instead. The more he thought about it, the more he became hopeful of a breakthrough. Bowlers were creatures of habit, and for Paddy to suddenly drop playing at his favourite rink was worthy of investigation. Paddy, or even when he was James Paisley, had always been a very considered and calculating person; almost predictable. This was an anomaly, which needed to be looked into.

He pulled into the car park, in the depressing dark of a December's late afternoon. He had just finished a call with Chas, who had updated him on the Benidorm theory. Like Chas, he felt it was a dead end, but nevertheless encouraged Dana to check with Alison on the possible involvement of her husband in the murder.

As luck would have it, there was a club Christmas competition, which had just started. It was something akin to the 'Fabulous Fives' competition at Daventry. Teams of five players had been drawn out of a hat. What went on then was a set of continuous team games, either pairs, triples or rinks. It was strictly time controlled, with a five-minute leeway being provided to allow the next games to start on time. The leaderboard at the far end of the rink, was key to the process, giving the scores and warning the players in the next matches to be ready. Cliff watched on in stunned admiration as chaos appeared to be well and truly organised. He thought NASA Mission Control would have been needed, but it was all in the capable hands of two octogenarians, maybe husband and wife – lovers if not -who were dextrously using two laptops to both input scores and move things smoothly along. All in all, there were sixty players, about ten facilitators – probably committee members - and four people manning the bar. Those currently not playing were either watching, supporting their team, or raiding the ample buffet.

Cliff recognised a former county rinks teammate in the shape of Reg Harrison and went over to talk to him. After giving a quick explanation of the task at hand, Reg led Cliff across to the side of rink number 1, where a grey-haired man, wearing a blazer, was viewing one of the games. Having whispered something in the guy's ear, Reg introduced Cliff to Damien Bryant, the club President. Damien looked at the picture Cliff showed him, and instantly recognised Paddy as being a previous two-time Desborough open winner. Apart from that he couldn't recall anything more of him, than being a worthy winner and seemingly nice guy.

Damien was more than happy for Cliff to ask those present about their recollections of Paddy. His only concern was that it didn't interfere with the timings of the games being played. With twenty minutes still remaining of the current matches, Cliff meticulously started working his way around those seated at the buffet tables. He would start there and move on to the ones spectating afterwards.

Quite a few remembered Paddy, commenting on his bowling prowess, and a few of the more bored members, who had previously played against either Paddy or Cliff, tried to engage him in conversation. With his eyes constantly on the large LED clock, Cliff managed to complete the task on time, and, somehow, without appearing rude by shutting down a conversation too sharply. He was even able to consume a much needed few sausage rolls and a glass of orange juice.

With half of the players now having been spoken to, Cliff used the changeover time to speak to the bar staff. Again, no luck. Cliff now had to pin his hopes on those that had just come off the rinks. He was getting tired and part of him wished the scoreboard were a big screen that he could project the picture of Paddy onto. No such luck.

With only two tables of people to go, his fortune did change.

'Yes, I do remember him,' said a fat balding man, after he put on his reading glasses to be sure. 'He was the guy that old Donny had a weird conversation with.'

'What do you mean?' Cliff enquired; his interest piqued.

'This guy had just received the trophy for winning the open, and Donny said to me while we were standing at the bar sipping our pints, "I think I know him". I thought nothing of it. Old Donny was always a one for telling stories.'

'So, what happened?'

'Well, the guy came up to the bar and stood right next to us, waiting to be served. So Donny says to him, 'I know you. You used to live in Derry. I'm sure it's you.'

'So, Donny was Irish?'

'Yeah, from Northern Ireland. Moved here to escape the troubles. Don't blame him either.'

'How did Paddy respond to that?' Cliff was getting excited. This could be the link.

'He flatly denied it,' the man replied. 'But Donny wouldn't have any of it, going about him being the spit of the guy he remembered. Apart from the beard having gone, that is.'

'How did it end?'

'As I recall, the guy just turned and walked out. Didn't even stop to pay for the pint he had ordered,' he paused for a bit. 'Of course, that night ended badly for poor old Donny?'

'How so?'

'Killed. A hit and run, while walking home that very night. And just thirty yards from his house.' He turned and pointed to one of a set of pictures hanging on a wall next to the table; apparently a memorial wall. 'That's him. That's Donny.'

Cliff read the name under the picture of a clean-shaven white-haired man proudly dressed in the now familiar Desborough Blazer. Liam O'Donovan.

'O'Donovan?' Cliff asked, needing confirmation. This was no coincidence.

'Yes, he had a large family. Big supporters of the bowls club, all of them. Sadly, none have stayed in the area. One of them was even working the bar that night, and…'

Cliff interrupted him. 'So that person could have overheard the conversation?'

The man nodded. Within five minutes, Cliff had a full history and description of that particular family member.

He thanked the man and, having left him money to buy a fresh pint, turned to leave. He needed to get outside as soon as possible. He knew, just as in

Daventry Bowling club, he'd struggle to have a phone signal. As he was walking towards the exit, he still had the good manners to look around to acknowledge Reg Harrison and Damien Bryant, thanking them for their help.

Outside there was an agonising wait for a few seconds. Finally, the BT icon in the top left corner changed from 'emergency' to show a three-bar reception. He had two urgent calls to make, and he had already decided in which order to do them.

Chapter 26

Roy couldn't believe his luck as he led Judith towards the bedroom. The afternoon had been taken up in preparation for the date, with his mind solely focused on getting everything right for his guest. The first thing he had done was to use his 'Braun-all-in-one' facial trimmer to get his goatee down to its optimal length, short enough to make sure no crumbs get lodged in the beard, but long enough to ensure the lady might quiver with excitement as he explores and stimulates her bikini area. He had starved himself of garlic for the past 24 hours. Nevertheless, he had brushed and flossed his teeth at least three times since he had woken up. He had found out early on, much to his frustration, that one-sided garlic breath could be a real passion killer.

In the bedroom, he had swapped his Liverpool FC duvet set for a freshly washed pastel one depicting the outlines of plants and trees. The alpine fabric softener he had specially purchased for the aforementioned wash, along with the output from the fresh scented humidifier he had 'borrowed' from Cliff's bedroom, made the room smell clean and inviting. At least he hoped so.

When it had come to selecting his wardrobe for the evening, he had thought long and hard about his choice of underwear. Initially, he had chosen a sleek black and gold Tanga brief. One where the elastase-cotton mix would beautifully display his goods. He had second thoughts when he was standing in front of the full-length mirror, as his stomach seemed to be overhanging more than he would like. Eventually, he plumped for a similar colour palette, but from his bamboo trunk collection. His prominence was still to the fore, but with the larger style of the trunk somehow minimising the overhang. Being made from bamboo, it was also an interesting topic for discussion, should he need to slow down his excitement. Casual light chinos, with a classy leather belt to match his slip-on loafers, and an open-necked Hawaiian shirt finished the look

He had invited Judith to drinks and nibbles. He was actually a good cook, but nibbles wouldn't clutter the room with dirty plates requiring washing-up, nor overfill the body. Also, he had ensured there were low-alcohol drinks on offer. Sildenafil, even at max strength, found its Kryptonite in excessive alcohol. At the age of 73, he certainly now needed a sexual tailwind to get him over the finishing line.

Any doubts he had, disappeared when he hung Judith's raincoat on the peg and turned to offer her a drink. She looked gorgeous. If not dressed to kill, she was dressed to thrill. She had her hair down, so that it framed her face perfectly. She was wearing makeup, but not too much. The ruby red colour of her lipstick, accentuated her mouth making it look as if it were perpetually screaming 'come kiss me' to Roy. She had carefully chosen a rather figure-hugging black dress. Figure hugging around her midriff, but figure freeing for the bosom. Roy couldn't take his eyes off her. He knew she was good looking, but that evening, in the annex alone with her, he was literally stunned by her beauty.

Judith accepted a glass of Prosecco, and together they sat slightly apart on the settee while the small talk flowed. Roy was thankful that the Amuse-bouche collection seemed to satisfy. With Christmas just around the corner, some shelves in Waitrose were already full of such seasonal goodies. He was just getting up to fetch the bottle for a refill, when he felt her pull him back down onto the sofa, with her right hand starting to stroke his inner thigh. Roy was slightly taken aback, well for a split second anyway. He was normally the one to make a move, to lean in, to separate the woman's lips with his tongue. This time, it was Judith that did all this, and he didn't mind at all.

The lead changed, however, when Roy who, due to an aching back, decided it was time to move onto the next level. So, he stood up and led her gently by the hand to his bedroom.

The bijou bedroom in the annex was beautifully decorated, according to Cliff's excellent taste. The bed itself was positioned slightly off-centre, being closer to the window than the en-suite. The smaller space between the bed and the wall just had room for a bedside table, with an alarm clock and angle-poise lamp on it. Between the bed and the en-suite was a single armchair. Roy normally used this as a dumping spot for his clothes when he was going to bed. He slept in his birthday suit, of course. There was no wardrobe in the small room; it wasn't big enough. The even tinier adjacent box room was used instead as an open plan clothes closet and dressing room.

Roy stopped in front of the armchair and started passionately kissing Judith once more. He skilfully unzipped her dress so it slid down her slender legs not stopping until it hit the floor. At the same time, Judith started to undress Roy. When he was just in his trunks, and Judith was left only wearing her matching teal lace lingerie, she slid under the duvet and beckoned Roy to her.

Roy, who prided himself as being the king of foreplay, started to nibble her neck and earlobes. Then, urged on by the gentle whimpering coming from Judith, he removed her delicate lace bra. The whimpering became loud gasps as the goatee went to work on Judith's obviously sensitive nipples. Judith was stimulating Roy with her gossamer touch, teasing him as she touched around his genitals, but always moving off to another spot rather than touch him there. Roy was very aroused now, and his right hand went down in search of that special small mound hidden under the other piece of teal coloured clothing.

However, as his hand made contact with its target, he felt Judith stiffen and then his hand was gently pulled up onto his own chest.

'Easy Roy,' she said, twirling the grey hairs next to his left nipple. 'I don't do this sort of thing lightly. I need to know that we both have genuine feelings for each other. I want commitment, and you haven't been around much recently.'

'I know love, it's the investigation. Cliff called this afternoon. He reckons we are getting really close.'

He then cocked his head and affected a moderately good impersonation of Humphrey Bogart. 'Then it's just you and me kid.'

Judith smiled and nibbled Roy's nearest nipple. 'That's what I wanted to hear.' With that, she sprang out of bed. 'If you like these,' she added, pointing to her knickers, 'then I've something in my handbag that will really knock you out.' She shut the door behind her. 'No peeking.' Roy heard her yell.

Roy closed his eyes for a few seconds, imagining Judith in a thong, a basque or even better a pair of crotchless edible panties. He raised the duvet, putting his head underneath, and then lifted the waistband of his trunks. 'Yes, the old boy is ready and raring to go,' he thought,

He heard the door open. 'I've got to look. I can't wait,' he said lowering the duvet. Instead of seeing Judith, amorously attired, there was an angry large man dressed in black. At first Roy didn't see the hammer raised in the man's left hand. He was looking at his face instead. The beard was gone, the head not now fully shaved, but the scar was undeniably still there, above his right eye. The last time he had seen this man, he had been pointing a gun at Roy in the streets of Derry. It was Micky O'Donovan.

O'Donovan clearly wanted to press home the advantage he had, having seen the shocked look on

Roy's face. In a swift move, aimed at keeping Roy out of the en-suite, he stepped, hammer still held high, towards the gap between the bed and the open bathroom door, whilst simultaneously using his lower body to push the left corner of the bed into the wall. Roy had instinctively started to get out of the bed on that side.

He soon realised that, while he had managed to distance himself a bit from O'Donovan, and gain time, his only potential exits meant either vaulting the corner of the bed or trying to run across it when O'Donovan made his move. Neither alternative seemed likely to have a positive outcome. The bed, being king size, did mean he was too far away for the hammer to do any damage. For the time being anyway.

O'Donovan was now almost level with Roy; his face puce with adrenaline and anger. This man wasn't going to show any leniency. He started to push against the bed once more, making the channel of escape even narrower. It was becoming like a murderous cat and mouse game, with Roy being the mouse. He chanced a glance back at the bedside table, looking for some weapon. Some hope. Knowing it was probably going to be in vain, he went to pick up the alarm clock. Having been a fine cricketer in his day, he decided to aim at Micky's head. As quick as it left his right hand, the velocity slowed to a stuttering halt as the alarm stalled, halfway across the bed, like an aircraft in distress, and dropped like a stone onto the duvet. Roy hadn't taken into account the fact it wasn't battery powered, and once the power lead had reached it maximum length, so had the flight of the flying alarm clock. The disappointed Roy then heard two more plopping sounds. His mind made sense of them straightaway; the louder being the plug falling out of its socket and landing on the carpet and the other being the connector falling gently onto the duvet.

O'Donovan laughed loudly. 'How the feck have you survived so long? You old git.'

He started to ease himself onto the bed, one knee at a time. Roy, pillow in front of his chest, primed himself for the onslaught. Were it not such a lethal situation, it could have appeared comical. A man, intent on murder, edging his way on his knees across the bed towards a semi-tumescent septuagenarian, dressed only in black and gold boxers, who is trying to fend the assailant off with a John Lewis pillow. To any onlooker, old enough that is, it was something akin to a game in 'It's A Knockout'.

They both turned to the door as a voice yelled. 'Get on with it. We have to get the other two tonight as well.' It was Judith, now dressed in black jogging bottoms and black hoodie. The fierceness in her tone was matched by the mania in her eyes. Suddenly those desirable red lips separated to show her teeth, and although they now seemed even more moist than before, they had now completely lost their appeal. Roy's mind conjured a dark image of a she-wolf ripping organs from its prey.

    O'Donovan started swinging the hammer like a man possessed. The pillow deflected some of the blows, but Micky - now aiming more at the sides of the pillow - struck Roy's left hand. He screamed in pain, subconsciously letting go with that hand. It fell back onto the anglepoise lamp. Roy had an idea. As Micky swung the hammer back, hoping to inflict more pain with the next blow, Roy tugged the lamp out of its power connector, while pushing the bed away from himself with his thighs. Micky lost his balance as he started his downswing, and toppled forward. Roy anticipating this, and using his right hand, now not encumbered by holding the pillow either, swung the lamp with all of his might. He caught Micky square on his left temple, making him fall further towards the foot of the bed.

    Having had to escape bedrooms, similarly attired and in almost as dangerous a circumstance, many times before, Roy instinctively performed a western roll across the bed. As he was mid-roll, he saw an arm go around Judith's neck and, as if in a David Copperfield magic show, she disappeared. His legs landed Olga Korbut like, a perfect 10, on the floor, allowing him to race into the en-suite, locking the door behind him.

Wishing he were in a film-star's house, rather than Cliffs small annex, so that he could use the 'bathroom phone' to call the police or, even better, be safely locked up in a panic room, he sat with his back braced against the bath and legs pushing against the door. He knew he had won a small battle, but feared the war was nowhere near over. This wasn't the Swiss border he had crossed, but a tiny foxhole with Panzers approaching.

His breathing was remarkably shallow, as he waited for the door to be breached. However, apart from some muffled angry noises, nothing happened. Eventually as the noises subsided, there was a gentle tap at the door, accompanied by a familiar male voice.

Chapter 27

'We should have been called 'Subparr' not them,' said Roy bitterly, as he looked at the people celebrating on the table next to him. 'Who bowls in an Argyll sweater anyway? He should receive a written warning for improper dress.'

'And a Merry Christmas to you, Roy 'the Grinch' Grimble,' laughed Cliff, taking a sip of his Bucks Fizz. 'Davy and Shirley epitomise all that is good about this wonderful club. If he wants to show his love of over sixty years for her by wearing that home-crafted,' he paused, 'albeit ill-fitting tent, then that is fine by me.' The Parrs, together with their team mates, Tel Boy Filler - another who would do anything he could to help anybody - and Johnny Mawe - a former TT motor cycling champion -, were pulling their luxury M&S crackers to reveal what their prizes for winning were.

Cliff and Roy had teamed up with club champion, Mick Wartherton and Murray Ferryman to play in the Christmas Rinks Sprint Knockout cup. With such a strong grouping they had been favourites to win the luxury crackers. However, just like all the other teams, who had been knocked out in the rounds before, they had been awarded another cracker; a much smaller one from Aldi.

Roy and Mick pulled a cracker, with Roy for once being the victor. He reached down and picked up a green plastic whistle. He put it to his mouth, and blew and blew. 'What's the bastard use of this?' he moaned, 'There isn't even a ruddy pea inside.'

Chas, who had been dropped off earlier by Dana before going off to do some Christmas shopping, was trying not to laugh. His ribs couldn't take it. 'Don't,' he wheezed. 'Maybe it's a magic whistle.'

'Magic, my arse. Cheap tat from China. Look at that,' he said pointing at the Subparrs, they've all got single malt miniatures from their crackers.'

'You might have too,' chimed in Mick, in his usual gruff tones, 'if you had bowled with your proper hand.'

'I did,' countered Roy indignantly. But then his riposte stopped, as he recognised the sarcasm.

With the bowling over, Marjory Deans declared the buffet open. Everyone had brought food or drink with a value of up to £5, and while the Sprint Rinks had been going on, she and Brend Walliams had been laying the foodstuff out on the tables. Their husbands, Philander and Raymond, the creators of the Bucks Fizz - the non-alcoholic version rather unimaginably being just orange juice - were in charge of distributing the drinks. The previous year it had been a self-service bar, but that didn't work out too well. Some people, not mentioning any names – well maybe just one, Roy Grimble - had been over generous with their self-allocation.

....

When they were all back at the table, and starting to tuck in, Murray turned to Roy.

'So, you thought you were a goner?'

He had only had the barest of outlines on their progress during the entire investigation, and when he caught the gist of what had happened in the annex, he felt guilty. After all, he was the one who had given them the keys to Paddy's house in the first place. Cliff told Murray to think no such thing. They were the ones who had wanted to help solve the murder of their friend much before that.

'Well, laying there with my legs pressed against the door, I wasn't too confident I'd survive,' Roy replied. 'When I recognised the voice coming from the bedroom, I could have cried.'

'You are lucky my daughter likes hunky men.' Cliff was smirking.

'When I was sure it was Adam, I unlocked the door and peeked out. I could have kissed him when I saw O'Donovan trussed up like a Christmas turkey on the bed.'

'With all the Viagra you'd probably taken, I bet Adam was glad you didn't.'

'How did they know to be there?' Murray asked.

'Old Casanova there had put his phone on silent, so missed my call from Desborough. I knew he was seeing Judith that evening, and alerted Sam. With Adam for support, they drove like the clappers to get to the house as soon as possible. Back up having already been summoned.'

'Did they have to break down the door?' asked Chas, thinking of the possible insurance claim.

'No,' replied Roy, 'When Judith went out to 'slip into something more comfortable…'

'Or more sexy, you thought.' Cliff couldn't suppress his joy at this part of the story. Obviously, it could have ended in tragedy, but as it turned out, it would be a story to be retold time and again. There is nothing better than having such a lurid story over one of your best mates.

'As I was saying. When she left the bedroom, she opened the door to let O'Donovan in. She needed to get dressed, so I guess between them they forgot to shut the front door.'

'Or didn't bother,' added Murray. 'So, Adam and Sam just walked in.'

'Probably a mistake they will regret for a very long time,' mused Cliff. 'Adam went in first and, catching Judith unawares, pulled her back into the lounge before throwing her to the floor. He then went into the bedroom after O'Donovan. Being a fireman, he is a strong man, but with O'Donovan already dazed from Roy's blow with the lamp, it was a relatively straightforward job to fully incapacitate him. Meanwhile, Judith was no match for Sam either.' Cliff was beaming with pride.

'I know she is a police officer,' said Roy, having just taken a sip of his beer, 'but does she always carry so many zip ties with her? If so then, a, Adam is lucky and, b, can I have some?'

Murray being used to Roy's silliness, asked a more sensible question. 'She has confessed, hasn't she? To Paddy's murder I mean.'

'Initially, it was "no comment" from both of them,' replied Cliff, 'but forensic evidence soon made them realise the inevitability of a conviction.'

'What did they have?'

'Stupidly, she gave O'Donovan the hammer she had used on Paddy. The autopsy on Paddy showed there were two blows leading to his death. The initial one which put him down was with the hammer. She then used one of his bowls nearby to finish him off, in the hope it might disguise the use of the hammer first. That didn't work, nor did she clean the hammer sufficiently to get rid of Paddy's DNA.'

'Thus making it the murder weapon,' said Chas. 'You said, she. Why couldn't it have been Micky O'Donovan?'

'The police in Belfast have CCTV images of Micky taking money out of an ATM there. On that very night.'

'I still don't understand why she'd kill Paddy,' Murray pushed. 'It all sounds so premeditated.'

'It was,' said Cliff sighing. 'It's a sad story really. Judith had a healthy and happy childhood, apart from one major event.'

'What was that?'

'Her twin brother, Ciaran, died of pneumonia when he was six.'

'That must have been terrible for her,' commented Murray. 'Losing a sibling, at any age is traumatic, but a twin when so young.'

'Apparently, it hit her hard, but she was in a loving family and she learned to move on. The best she could anyway. The turning point in her life was her eighteenth birthday when she was told the truth.'

'The truth about what?' Chas asked. Cliff hadn't had time to fill the others in fully, so this was as new to him as it was to Murray. Roy, as Cliff's lodger and being there at the time of arrest, knew a lot more of the story than Chas.

'Her father, or the man she grew up calling "dad", told her that her real parents had been killed by the British army in Derry when she was a baby, and that he and his wife were in fact her uncle and aunt.'

Cliff then told his assembled friends, in great detail, how that day turned Judith into a murderer. Judith, once she recovered from the shock, wanted to know everything about her biological parents and what had happened. She learned about the man who lodged with her parents, Padraig O'Toole. The way he had abused their hospitality, spying on them and reporting back to the occupying forces. The more she heard about the troubles and the way the Catholic people were treated, the more she became radicalised. O'Toole became a demon in her eyes as she learned that he was very likely responsible for the dawn raid. She even laid the death of her brother at his door. Ciaran, like her, was a healthy baby, but after being left on the doorstep the morning of the raid, he started to develop chest issues, which only got worse as he got older.

She wanted to go over to Derry to fight for the cause, but that was just as The Good Friday Agreement came into being. Her aunt, the woman she grew up calling mum, was instrumental in turning her away from that path. She cited the brave women of Northern Ireland, on both sides, who had campaigned so long and so hard. 'We need to respect them. They have suffered so much, and lost so many' she argued. Judith, seeing the way the tide was turning away from direct action, calmed somewhat in the light of her aunt's reasoning.

She started working behind the bar at Desborough bowls club in the evening, while studying catering management at Tresham College in Kettering. The evening of the Open competition, she witnessed the exchange between her uncle and the man from Daventry who had won the trophy. She had been looking at the man, who she later found out was called Paddy Cullen, when her uncle suggested he knew him from Derry. For the briefest of moments, she had seen a look of fear in his eyes. After the man had rushed away, ignoring the pint she had just poured for him, she asked her uncle about it.

When the twins were born, her uncle and aunt had gone over to Derry for the christening. The ensuing party had been very raucous, with lots of drink consumed, so her uncle's memory was a bit hazy. He did remember their lodger, Paisley, had vacated his room for them, and was staying with a friend for those few days. He recalled a small group of the guys present had been playing hurling before the christening. They were sitting together in the dining room at the party. The guy from Daventry looked like the guy he bumped into when he was coming out of the toilet. He only really remembered him as they did "that dance"; the one where you both step to the side, but in the same direction and therefore can't pass one another. Judith asked her uncle there and then whether he was Paisley. He could only shake his head saying, 'Paisley was probably one of those guys, but I'm not even sure he was the one I bumped into. He had dark hair and a bit of a beard then'.

Judith had stayed to clear the bar and lock up, otherwise she would have been walking home with her uncle when he was run over and killed. Had that been the case, being sober herself, she was confident her wonderful uncle would still have been alive. Once the grief, and slight guilt, had started to subside, she allowed herself to revisit the thought that he really was Paisley. She kept seeing the look of fear in his eyes, and slowly she formulated a theory that he had been the driver of the car. It made sense if he were. A hell of a coincidence if he weren't.

She reached out to her cousin in Belfast, Micky O'Donovan, asking him if he knew, or could find out, anything about Paisley. A few days later, she received a couple of photos, taken at the christening. Micky, after asking everyone he could, had then used a red marker pen to circle the same man in both photos. Unfortunately, as he wasn't the subject of either photo, his image was blurry in each one. Try as she might, using a scanner and any software her college friends could suggest, his face remained out of focus, with little or no defining features. There were, however, enough similarities in their general look for her not to give up.

'So, she moved here to Daventry to be near to him,' said Chas. 'Talk about playing the long game. She must have been here almost two years.'

'Yes, I suppose if she were going to get revenge and kill him,' Cliff paused for a second before continuing, 'then she wanted to be sure.'

'How very decent of her,' said Roy sarcastically.

'Once here, she tried to bump into Paddy as much as possible. Asking a question here, probing there. But, despite being friendly, even chatty, he gave nothing away.'

'What did she do then?' Murray asked.

'She decided she needed to get into Paddy's bungalow. She knew he lived alone. So, she told him she was struggling financially, and asked whether he needed a cleaner.'

'Very devious,' observed Roy. 'What did I ever see in her?'

'Mammary glands,' answered Chas, who swiftly wished he hadn't said that because the resulting belly laugh caused his ribs to pain.

'Paddy wasn't keen at first, but did invite her around to allow her to cost the work. Once inside, she offered to do a trial clean, ensuring she'd be left alone. She was beginning to think she was on the wrong track with Paddy, when she saw the bowls trophy from Derry in the cabinet. Then she knew.'

'The trophy gave him away,' commented Chas. 'A rare act of vanity and carelessness on his part.'

'Anyway,' continued Cliff, knowing his story was almost over, 'she waited a few days, before turning up unexpected. She explained her situation had worsened and wondered whether he might know of one or two others who might want a cleaner. Although he was only wearing his dressing gown and slippers after a shower, Paddy invited her into the conservatory where he was putting new competition stickers on his bowls. As he was bending over to clear stuff from a chair for her to sit on while he went to get dressed, she seized the moment and hit him on the head with the hammer she had brought in her bag. He fell to his knees, on the verge of losing consciousness, so she cleverly picked up the nearest bowl and, with two hands, hit him as hard as she could in exactly the same spot. The force of that second blow knocked him backwards onto the floor and finished him off. She then casually went on to make the crime scene look like it was a robbery gone wrong.'

'You almost have to admire her,' said Chas. 'She managed to overpower and kill an ex-SAS man.'

'She did have age, surprise and anger on her side,' responded Cliff.

'Why did she try to kill me though?' Roy asked, almost petulantly. 'And three bloody times.'

'According to Sam, she was peed off with O'Donovan and Ahern. The bomb was only supposed to be a warning. Ahern texted Micky to say you were in the pub, not realising Sinead had already left.'

'They didn't mean to kill Sinead then,' Roy was aghast. 'She died because of a mistake. Because of me.' Tears started to form in his eyes.

'Not because of you, Roy,' Chas said, patting Roy's arm. 'Not even because of us. It was all them.'

'Quite right. Unfortunately, she used you Roy. Your feelings for her. She used them to keep her informed about our progress.' Cliff smiled wanly at his friend. He realised it wasn't the best of things to be told.

'So, I almost got myself killed. Great.' Roy's doleful face, suddenly burst into a smile. 'Here they come. My brave heroes. And the bravest one of all. The one who has to put up with Chas 24/7.'

'Look who I bumped into in the car park,' said Dana, giving her husband a peck on the cheek. Chas, in the spirit of Christmas, decided to pucker up rather than strike back at Roy's cheap jibe.

'Hi guys,' said Sam, unwrapping a woolly scarf from around her neck. 'Adam and I are off to the emergency services' Christmas party….'

'Bloody Tory government,' interrupted a now more cheerful Roy. 'We haven't got enough police officers and fireman for them to have their own dos. Bastard cuts to the private sector.'

'Actually, we do,' countered Adam. 'We work together a lot, and it seems the right thing to do. Particularly at this time of year.'

'There was something I thought you'd like to know,' said Sam, changing the topic, not wanting to get into a political discussion with Roy.

'What is that luv?' Cliff asked.

'Well I've just seen Judith's DNA report. In layman's terms fifty percent of her DNA is the same as that of James Paisley.'

'The XX, XY tattoos on his body,' Chas announced. 'Judith and Ciaran.'

'That means Judith killed her biological father,' added Cliff. He paused for a few seconds, letting this bombshell sink in. 'No wonder he didn't want to risk leaving the twins in the house that morning.'

'I did hear rumours that Mary O'Donovan was not very happy in Derry,' said Roy. 'She must have turned to Paisley.' He paused, then…'Does Judith know? This will fuck her up even more.'

And any antipathy Roy had been feeling towards Judith melted.

Epilogue

Cliff sat sipping a cappuccino, glancing every couple of minutes at the arrivals screen off to his right. Ordinarily, he hated picking up people from Heathrow, but terminal 5 was that bit more accessible and that bit less crowded. Having parked in the short stay car park, he (almost!) felt relaxed when the board announced that Alejo's flight was delayed. After all, it had been over four months since they had been together. Four months of Skype calls and cold showers. Did that mean love?

Two weeks earlier, Cliff had driven Chas and Dana to terminal 4. Chas had recovered fully, and ahead of time. Under Dana's tender and attentive care, could the outcome ever have been in doubt? One of the factors which had contributed to his speedy rehabilitation was the joint desire for them to visit their son, James, who had emigrated to Brisbane five years previously. Even though this trip meant a break in the agreed biennial visit, their near-death experience at the hands of Etches and Bull made them doubly determined to enjoy life to the full. The most surprising thing for Cliff was that the ever price conscious Chas didn't baulk at the extortionate cost of the flights. In the light of the recent investigation, the irony was obvious to both Chas and Dana. A murder linked to the theft of gold, which had almost led to their demise, meant they were hell bent on going to the Gold Coast.

Dana, the female apple of Cliff's eye, had given Cliff a timetable of chores to carry out for them while they were away. Chores which Cliff happily carried out for his friends. He had, however, resolved to add an item to that list. One which would cause Dana's cheeks to redden, should she ever find out. For years Cliff had wondered what really lay in that games' cupboard. So, when he went there to water the indoor plants and feed the perpetually dormant cat, he had gone straight to the cupboard only to have his excitement immediately thwarted when he saw a shiny, obviously brand new, padlock straddling the handles. 'Good for them,' Cliff had thought. 'We all need our secrets.'

The atmosphere in the car two weeks earlier, when Cliff had acted as chauffeur for his friends, had been light and cheerful. The trip to Australia, as well as being a much-needed filial visit, was a symbolic full stop to everything that had gone on before. Only ten days earlier, the seemingly never-ending trials had come to an end. The last one being that of Bull and Etches. Initially, it looked like being a very protracted affair with Bull looking to plead not guilty to all charges. This was despite the fact that Etches' had signed his confession, fully implicating Bull, and was therefore not going to contest the prosecution's evidence.

However, Bertie, now back from his Caribbean cruise, had saved the day. Chas had previously only ever seen a calm and controlled Bertie, but when he was catching Bertie up on how the investigation had progressed, including the home invasion, he thought Bertie was going to blow a gasket. Ever the gentleman, he was incensed by the thought of Dana having to relive the assault in court, and being subjected to a cross-examination to boot. Chas had naturally been sketchy about the details, but Bertie was aware of the charges Bull was facing and feared the worst. Without saying anything to Chas, he called Mike Wilkes and together they hatched a plan.

Chas and Dana were delighted, a few days later, when the CPS informed them that Bull was changing his plea to guilty, including the sexual assault. This meant Dana wouldn't have to give evidence at the trial after all. The reason for this change of heart by Bull only came to light when Chas bumped into Bertie in a garden centre and told him the good news. Bertie hadn't seemed surprised in the least. Because he had been so angry before, his blasé reaction confused Chas at first.

'Did you have a hand in it?' Chas asked, not really seeing how Bertie could have been involved. But the question slipped almost unbidden off his tongue. The thought had entered Chas' mind, so it needed to be asked.

Bertie smiled. 'Well, we did point out to him that his actions on Tierra del Fuego were illegal. That would mean a retrospective court martial and dishonourable discharge.' He paused before continuing. 'Not only would he lose his army pension after his release, the army would seek recompense for any money he had received since he left the service.'

'So, you offered him a deal?' Chas asked. 'He wouldn't be held to account for his actions down there if he pleaded guilty.'

'Well, if you take into account the fact that he was bang to rights anyway,' Bertie replied, 'then he had no choice. He might as well look to his future welfare.'

At the end of the trial, the judge showed Etches no leniency, despite his deal with the CPS, and he was sentenced to eight years in jail. Bull, on the other hand due to the sexual nature of one of the charges, received a total of eleven years with the judge saying that he wished he could have made his stay a lot longer.

A month earlier, Judith's trial had taken place. Everyone was a little surprised that it hadn't been held at the Old Bailey, but given the circumstances, Northampton Crown Court in Lady's Lane sufficed.

Judith had initially broken down when she found out she had killed her father. However, being confined to a cell allows you to mull things over. Paisley wasn't really her father. Her uncle and aunt had been her true parents. He had merely taken advantage of a sad and lonely woman. Had they not been killed, she might have grown up calling the O'Donovan's mum and dad. But Paisley's actions had not only caused their demise, they had also triggered the chain of events which caused her beloved twin brother to die prematurely. On reflection, Paisley/Cullen being her biological father made no difference to her. She felt he deserved to die and she was happy to have been the one to find justice for everyone who had suffered because of his deceitful behaviour. Nonetheless, she was somewhat remorseful. She had allowed her emotions to get the better of her, particularly the one for self preservation. Sinead shouldn't have died, even if that were an accident, and it was wrong to have tried to have poor Roy killed. The domino effect of this meant that it wouldn't have stopped there. Chas and Cliff would have had to have been silenced as well. Lying on her thin mattress in the cell, Judith bitterly regretted her actions after the murder of Paisley. So much so that she reached out, through her solicitor, to Roy. She was disappointed, but not surprised, when word came back that he wouldn't come and visit her in jail. 'Maybe in time?' Judith hoped.

Judith's trial was short, but certainly not sweet. She pleaded guilty and, in line with the sentencing rules in the UK, received a mandatory life sentence. Her judge, Sir William Phillips, referred to her tragic story when setting the minimum sentence as low as possible, at fifteen years. 'A life has been taken. We must remember that. The murder itself was calculated and premeditated. However, this woman has been suffering and agonising since she was made aware of the facts about her past. She now has at least fifteen years to prove whether she can be an asset to the community once more.'

    Cliff took another sip of his coffee and looked, once more, at the arrival's screen. Judging by the predicted arrival time, Alejo would be coming through that sliding door in about twenty minutes. Every time they had spoken since the arrest, Alejo had always felt it necessary to thank Cliff. Cliff hated it, but accepted that their relationship was still in a fledgling state. After Alejo passed on Cliff's information regarding the missing gold from Tierra del Fuego, the Argentinian authorities had not only arrested Taffy Evans, but shut down a global mineral smuggling ring. Apparently, the resourceful Taffy, had broadened his customer base. Frustrated by the infrequent biennial nature of Paddy's requirements, he had used his contacts to find other clients wishing to export other illicitly-acquired metals in a forged state. Taffy, not wanting to spend any more time than necessary in an Argentinian jail, had turned state's evidence and consequently three of the country's major criminal gangs had been implicated, with arrests made and convictions secured. For sure, Alejo had earned a lot of brownie points.

'Not long now,' thought Cliff. The information that the plane had landed had appeared five minutes earlier. His heart began to race with excitement. In an effort not to greet his lover in a sweaty state, he let his mind wonder towards Roy. Although he wouldn't admit it, that evening in the annex had shaken Roy in more ways than one. He became withdrawn for a while, seemingly having lost his usual self-confidence. For a week or two, he avoided going anywhere unless it was with Cliff. It was his landlord who came up with the answer. Under the ruse of taking him to a bowls shop in Nottingham, for retail therapy, Cliff surprised Roy by turning into East Midlands airport. His confusion turned to delight when he saw Michael Kelly waiting at the pick-up point.

Cliff soon found out why Roy had taken to Michael so much. His positivity and kindness were infectious. Roy was back to being his old self in no time, and when they were dining at Chas' one night, his ears had pricked up when he heard Dana telling Michael about Alison in Spain. The fact that she was still married, even if it were unhappily so, didn't deter Roy. The way he viewed it was, where there is an attractive and sexually frustrated woman, he could be the one to provide the comfort and support needed. Roy had spent the rest of that evening unsuccessfully badgering Dana for more details. Roy was undeterred. He knew he would wear Dana down eventually. When that happened, he would be on the plane to Spain.

Ironically, his next flight was to Belfast for the trial of O'Donovan. Cliff went too and they both stayed with Michael and his family. O'Donovan was found guilty of the manslaughter of Sinead and attempted murder of Roy, the latter on two counts. His sentence of twenty years was a heavy one, but Roy still cries when he thinks of poor Sinead losing her life so unnecessarily. In his mind no sentence, no matter how severe, would be adequate. Nothing could ever bring Sinead back.

The one positive this investigation had achieved was friendship. Not only had the group in Daventry grown even closer, but new strong friendships had been forged, like the ones with Bertie and the Kellys. Smiling as he mused over this, Cliff saw the arrivals door open and through them stepped someone who melted his heart. As he and Alejo walked quickly towards one another, an image flashed into Cliff's mind.

A Shetland pony.

Acknowledgments

I came to write this book at a time of great internal conflict and emotional stress. I had been in two minds as to whether I was up to writing my first solo book. Fortunately, I have stronger and very supportive people around me, and the process of writing Wrong Bias became a form of therapy, allowing my mind to focus on something creative rather than the destructive thoughts continuously permeating in it.

To that end, I have many people to thank. Some who have been there for me over many years, and others who have allowed me to become their friends in the past year.

Firstly, I'd like to thank Andy, my old friend from school. As well as acting as my encouraging and hard-working editor, he suggested the link to Argentina in the planning stage of the book. Charles, Ray and Brenda, who all have acted as my test readers, have given their time willingly and their positive feedback has helped me develop my writing style and improve both the storyline and characters.

Finally, I'd like to mention the lovely members of Daventry Indoor Bowling Club and and Staverton Golf Club. The array of characters there and anecdotes they have shared made writing this book a joy, rather a chore. Any members, who have been the inspiration for elements of the characters within the book, of course have been made aware of this. They have all given me their approval and taken the news with either a degree of excitement or total indifference.

Cliff

Printed in Great Britain
by Amazon